# *A COWBOY FOR CHRISTMAS*

Kristen N. Bailey

*For Cathy
Hope you enjoy!
Thanks for joining the giveaway
Kristen James (Bailey)*

*Kristen N. Bailey*

# A Cowboy For Christmas

ISBN 978-0-9821755-9-0

Story © 2009 Kristen N. Bailey
www.kristen-bailey.com
admin@kristen-bailey.com

Artwork © Tandi Bregman
www.tandiventer.com

Other Novels by Kristen N. Bailey:
The Enemy's Son - Romantic Suspense
The River People - Young Adult Historical

Published by Brilliant Book Press

All incidents and characters are fictional, and any resemblance to any person or event, past or present, is coincidence.

Printed in the United States of America.

# Chapter One

If her name meant anything to the tall cowboy who leaned against the porch rail, he didn't react. Instead, he appraised her with sky blue eyes while the afternoon light slanted against him. She'd pulled up to the house and introduced herself, and now waited for his name or a hello.

"The name ain't ringing a bell," he said quietly, then looked her up and down. "And believe me, I'd remember your face."

*Would you now?* It sounded like a compliment, but he didn't smile with it. Missy wasn't sure what to make of him.

His voice carried like a gentle breeze. The man, however, looked rough as the landscape around them. Hard stance, set jaw, arms folded. His long, lean body might be perfect for pressing against a woman, but his eyes were distrusting.

The sign clearly said Ocean View Stables, so she knew she had the right place.

"Melissa Nelson," she repeated. This was awkward. "Ben may have called me Missy." Come on, nothing? She rubbed her arms through her jacket, chilled from the cool Oregon weather and this overly warm welcome. "I'm Ben's sister. Aren't you Mr. Hatcher?"

"Nope." He tilted his head and stared some more, like he'd never seen a woman before. The daylight darkened. Raindrops plopped on her while she waited for some kind of answer. Any kind of answer would be nice. "Ben's lawyer called you," he added, "And you came right over. I see."

He wore a tan Stetson on his head, a rich blue shirt with sleeves rolled up, snug Wranglers, and boots. He'd make a great bedroom poster, something to ogle on lonely nights, but his too sexy look only distracted her.

Did she really lose her train of thought while checking him out? "I flew in from Nevada . . . He asked me to come." She almost added that Mr. Hatcher was supposed to meet her here. Wouldn't this guy know that?

"Come on in, then." Without introducing himself, he turned to the front door and led the way in. Inside, she fought off a shiver. It wasn't the cold this time, but a reaction to his nearness. His eyes were so intent on her, she could scarcely breathe.

Scents of leather and pine met her inside his home. A man's home, for sure. "How did you know Ben?" she asked.

He opened a closet door and gestured to her coat. She wanted an answer, but decided to shrug out of her coat, since it was thin and wet anyway.

With his brows creased at her, he took it. "We went in fifty-fifty on this place."

Oh, no. She hadn't considered there would be other investors. That explained why he was here. "So you live here?"

"Yup." He faced her and rested his hands on his hips in a lazy manner. Irritated, she turned and glanced around at the open floor plan.

She spotted a kitchen nook off to her left. What kind of man had a kitchen nook? To her right, a fire smoldered in the large brick fireplace in the living room. What she could see of that room gave an impression of comfort, where a family could gather.

His house was beautiful, but it looked more like a family home than a bachelor's place. Well, it could be with some personal touches. At least it was warm and dry, unlike the misty weather outside.

Since he blocked her way, she couldn't ignore him any longer. "What?" The words burst out, and sounded desperate to her own ears.

"You look like him."

Well, he knew her late brother, but she didn't know enough about Ben's life to guess who this guy could be. She asked, "Were you close to my brother?"

"Friends, business partners," he said with a shrug as if it didn't matter.

He moved toward the kitchen, but turned back around and looked her over again. "Ben never talked about any sister."

*Ouch.* "Well . . . We weren't raised together. We didn't even know about each other until our father died three years ago." Since she could lose herself in the hurtful past, she tried to ignore it.

"Missed the funeral, you know." Arms folded, he leaned back against the counter. She couldn't pinpoint anything about him that would make a shiver race up her back, though one did.

"Ben's lawyer didn't get a hold of me until yesterday," she explained. He walked around the counter and into the kitchen, a tidy space decorated only with a lone marble horse statue on the counter.

Sighing, she rubbed her temples while his back was turned. He couldn't know she was jobless, with an uncertain future, and had spent a pretty penny on the airfare to come out.

She'd withdrawn some of her savings to make the trip. The lawyer wouldn't have asked her to come unless there was something here for her. Now she wondered if it would be worth it.

"I get it." He faced her, planted both hands on the counter, and leaned toward her. "You hoped to make out with some dough. Too bad you didn't know about me." He ignored her gasp and pulled several things from the refrigerator, then started lunch on the opposite counter, with his back to her.

"What kind of person says something like that? You don't know me!" Who cared if it might be true? He had no right to be so rude, not when he didn't know why she hadn't been able to get better acquainted with her brother.

"Exactly." He didn't turn around to speak. It appeared like he wanted her to leave. He added, "I don't know you. I knew Ben, and you never came to visit."

How could she have known they were out of time? "Listen, I don't have to explain myself to you. I was *asked* to come here, remember?"

No answer. *Figures.* She tapped the toe of her shoe as she sought another angle to try. "So who are you?"

His face, when he glanced back at her, had softened. Those blue eyes could melt a woman's will, but she doubted he'd use them on her. All the better, because she didn't need another man using her and then tossing her away.

"Brent Williams. Ben and I started this place together."

Brent meant the ranch, the hills and paths she'd seen when she drove in, and the horses that grazed and ran in the pastures. Maybe she'd get somewhere now. "Is the lawyer coming?"

"He's on his way over." He turned around and pushed a plate across the counter. "Might as well join me for lunch."

"Lunch?" At the word, her stomach growled. After the flight into Oregon and the drive west to Florence, she felt starved. She'd been too distracted to eat as she thought about the past and worried about her future. "Umm, thanks."

"You look like you need some good food in you." He poured her a glass of milk to go with it before he walked around the counter with a stool for her to sit on. She didn't know what to make of the sudden hospitality from the cold cowboy, but once she bit into the sandwich, she didn't care. "Wow."

He sat on a stool on the opposite side. They ate without discussion, and the passing minutes grew more tense.

When she couldn't take the silence, she asked, "How did Ben die? The lawyer didn't tell me."

Brent's gaze dropped down to the counter. "You can ask him when he gets here."

Okay, so no more playing nice. While he didn't look distraught over Ben's death, he sure closed up when she asked about it.

Why did he have to be so brutally attractive? Why was he rude to her, and then fixed her lunch? She contemplated his actions while she nibbled on the last of her sandwich.

He drained his glass and set his plate next to the sink, then stood in the kitchen and looked at her. And, boy, did he look at her. After he searched her face, his gaze slid down her throat. She tried to keep the color from her checks, thankful she hadn't worn anything low-cut.

"Are you sure Mr. Hatcher is on his way?" She couldn't take much more of this.

"Yeah, he called right before you showed up."

Now why didn't he mention that before? She glared. He glared back. Someone knocked.

"That'd be him." He left her trembling with anger and answered the door, where a middle-aged man in a suit waited. She stayed by the kitchen counter.

Brent greeted the shorter, dark haired man by saying, "Did you know Ben had a sister?"

"He mentioned some family," the other man said with an easy-going smile as he came in and offered a hand to Missy. "Nice to meet you in person, Miss Nelson. I'm Nick Thatcher. Looks like you found the place without problem."

"The problems started after I got here." She spoke coldly and threw a look at Brent.

Nick turned to Brent. "Are you giving her a hard time?"

Brent gave him a *what can I do?* shrug. Nick sighed and said, "Ah, he's rough on the outside, but he's a good man."

"You two are buddies?" she asked. Great, a big conspiracy.

"That doesn't mean anything bad for you, Miss Nelson." He looked at Brent and held up his briefcase. "Is there somewhere you'd like to sit down and go over this?"

Brent led the way into the living room. He sat on the couch across from her and sank back, his eyes once again on her like a hawk about to strike. Did he look at her because she reminded him of Ben, or did he think of the quickest way to get rid of her?

She took a deep breath and decided to pretend indifference. In reality, she hoped this would give her a way to start over, somewhere new. After her last relationship, and her job, crumbled, she needed direction.

"Ben left no children, as you both know, and no other relatives but you, Miss Nelson," Nick started. "As such, his interest in Ocean View Stables goes to you."

"No!" Brent sprang to his feet. "That's just not right. This is my ranch, built by my own sweat and blood. Ben's interest should go to me now."

Nick sat forward. "Now, hold on and let me talk. Miss Nelson didn't come here to take over your ranch. There's no reason why you can't buy her out."

That's what she wanted to hear. Brent glared at her as if she'd set the place on fire.

"Brent," Nick started, "Is there a possibility you can buy her out?"

Brent went to the window that overlooked the pastures outside and spoke. "We just got started two years ago, and we're not turning much of a profit yet. So, no, there isn't the capital to do anything like that."

Missy yanked in a breath. Now what? "What does that mean?"

Nick's brow furrowed and he puffed out his cheeks. "Well, you have half interest in these stables. Do you like horses?"

Brent spun around. "This is my place and it's staying that way."

Her and horses? Could today go any worse?

"I'm sorry, Brent, but you own the back forty acres. Miss Nelson now owns the front forty, along with Ben's six horses." Nick weaved his plump fingers together. She guessed he might be considering the options for them, but she didn't plan to sit back and let them decide.

"I can take over Ben's work here." Now where did that wonderful idea come from? Just because Brent didn't want her here didn't mean she had to stay and spite him. Did it?

Both men looked at her with blank faces. Okay, so maybe she should have dressed in something besides her silk suit. And stilettos.

Nick coughed, but it sounded suspiciously more like a laugh to Missy. "I don't think you understand what's involved in caring for horses. And what about your job back home?"

She wouldn't tell them, but that was the problem. She didn't have a job. "Do you think I'm not capable?"

She'd directed the challenge at Nick, but he looked down and shuffled his papers. Brent sat down on the couch and answered as he linked his fingers behind his head, "You're not needed."

"Oh, so you'll hire someone to take on Ben's share of the work?" The property seemed to be a good size, but she hadn't seen any other men who worked it.

He let out a pent-up breath.

*Ha, got you, don't I?*

"Miss Nelson, could you sign these papers now?" Nick stood and took them to the counter. Brent's insistent gaze kept her in her seat for a second. Thoughts of fighting with him every day unnerved her . . . and made her feel restless.

She broke their staring contest when she stood, and left Brent to stomp around and swear in his living room.

When she joined Nick at the counter, she asked in a whisper, "How did Ben die?"

After glancing toward the other room, he whispered, "A wreck on the freeway. He was pulling an empty horse trailer."

"How awful." She shivered and wished she could push the feelings away.

"Please don't ask Brent about it," he said, sparking her interest. She gave him a look she hoped would prompt him to explain, but Nick didn't elaborate. Instead he explained the papers and took her through page by page. He pointed and she signed.

"Thank you, Miss Nelson, I'll be in touch." He nodded to her and met Brent by the door. After he spoke with Brent, he waved and left. They stood next to each other, two strangers facing off.

"You obviously don't want me here. That's okay, I'm used to that." She folded her arms, and kept a calm demeanor despite the fear that he could tell her to leave at any moment.

He rubbed his chin, maybe thinking, and she noticed the way his shirt pulled over his muscles. He had a presence about him, like a graceful oak that presided over an otherwise treeless field.

But his good looks didn't mean a thing. So, what if one more man thought he could brush her aside? She had every right to stay. Ben had, after all, bought all this with the inheritance money from their father. Her father raised her, but he left everything to a son Missy had never even met.

"What do you know about horses?" he asked, and it threw her out of her thoughts. She pictured the horses she'd seen in parades. Maybe she shouldn't show off her expertise.

Brent sighed. "I see. So you've never ridden, but you want to come out here and play cowgirl."

This wasn't a game. "This is the only way I have to know Ben now."

He must have heard something in her voice, because he studied her again, this time with kinder eyes. "We have a lot of work to do around here."

"So I'll learn." She'd end up with every dirty job he didn't want, but she'd settle for that. "What else can we do?"

He didn't have a choice, and they both knew it.

"We take boarder horses, mostly in the winter." He surprised her when he switched into instructor mode. "We give lessons and take groups on rides over the hills and down to the beach. You'll have to learn how to ride and care for the animals."

"Okay." She'd adapted many times in her life, and she could do it now. "I just have one stipulation."

He looked at her with raised brows. "Go on."

"You can't stare at me like that," she said and folded her arms. His lips twitched and his cool eyes lightened for a second before his hard look returned.

He pulled her coat from the closet and handed it to her. "So if I stare at you all day, you'll leave?"

"Fat chance," she said before she slipped her coat on.

"Did you bring any bags with you?" he asked and actually looked away from her to open the front door.

"A suitcase."

"Well, I'll show you to Ben's. I guess it's yours now."

\* \* \* \*

Brent grabbed his suede jacket and headed out into the morning mist. The fog blocked his view of Ben's house farther down the road, but he still looked in that direction as he pictured Missy. Obviously Nez Pierce like her brother, she had reddish-cocoa skin and exotic brown eyes. They were huge and slightly tilted. Did she ever use them to seduce men?

More importantly, did she care about her dead brother? Care that she came here and replaced him?

What would a sweet little city slicker do out here without her morning espresso? She didn't exactly talk like someone from the city, but she dressed like one. He only knew she was from east of here.

He stalked down to the horse stables, but froze mid-step at the entrance. His Appaloosa gelding, Jeffery, nuzzled Missy's hand.

Thoughts of that darn woman had kept him up half the night. But she looked rested. What was she doing here so early?

Her face wasn't guarded. He hadn't realized just how snobby she'd looked the day before in her nice clothes, but now she smiled at the animal. Her hair hung down her back like a black, shinny mane. It'd been up yesterday, so he hadn't guessed it was so long.

Nick was wrong. She was here to take over the stables, starting with his own damn horse.

The traitor horse reacted to Missy just like he had to Ben. She had the same natural ease around them. They made a nice picture, for sure. That long body of hers would look great riding on a horse.

She must have listened to his suggestion that she go into town and buy some work clothes. Now in jeans, insulated boots, and a thick, winter coat, she looked like she could belong. On her own ranch, that was.

Wasn't it his luck that she was so hot? He loved long hair, and she had plenty. And huge brown eyes in an oval face. Lips that just begged for a kiss. Darn it, he didn't need to waste his time with fantasies.

She saw him and stepped back from the horse.

"Morning," he said as he rested a hand on the stall. "I see you and my horse are on good terms."

"What's his name?" Her gaze rested on the horse, then Brent, and then the horse again. A teasing smile slipped onto her face.

"His name's Jeffery. And what's so funny?" He caught himself right before he returned that enticing smile.

"They say pets and their owners start to look alike. Jeffery has your long face."

One corner of her mouth tilted up before she bit her lip. He saw her white teeth nibble on her lower lip and thought of doing the same. *Whoa!*

"So does Dancer remind you of Ben?" he asked, tilting his head to the black stallion that watched her.

Missy looked back at the wild-looking thing. "I don't know."

Yeah, he had her there. Funny thing was, he felt bad that he'd made her face go all sad. "So, you ready?"

She nodded, though she couldn't know what she agreed to.

"Great, truck's outside," he said and noticed how quiet she was. He waited until she slid in and buckled up to start the engine. Her lavender scent smelled strange mixed with the truck's normal leather smell. "Not a morning person?"

She shrugged.

"Missy?" That made her turn her face his way.

"Sorry, I've got so many things on my mind," she said, still not focused on him.

"Second thoughts about being here, or worries about the life waiting for you?"

"I'll pull my weight, don't worry. And I'm sticking around, so get used to me."

"Yes, ma'am." He turned the truck off his gravel road, onto the highway, and sped up.

"It's just being in Ben's house . . ." She looked down at her lap.

He felt guilty. Maybe he shouldn't have left her there alone. Too late now.

Or could he fix it? "I wasn't thinking. You can move over to my place if you need to." What in hell was he thinking now? *Her* in *his* house?

"It's all right. Being there just made me think about him more, wonder about him." She turned to her window, and a minute later, added, "The sky there looks like the inside of a seashell."

At her soft comment, he glanced over. She was too pretty to be sitting in his dusty truck. Something stirred in him at the sight of her hair, her hands resting one on top of the other in her lap. Casual beauty, he thought.

Darn it, her looks weren't his business.

A few days of hard ranch work, and she'd hit the road for home. Just like Amanda had two years before.

"We need more hay for the horses," he said. Since she still gazed out the side window, he let himself stare for a quick minute. Nice profile. Nice mouth, too. A man could go crazy thinking about kissing her. But back to ranch business . . . "There's two guys working out here, Dale and Ivan. You'll run across them."

"They live on the property?" she asked, and the hint of panic in her voice surprised him. So far, she acted as if nothing could run her off.

He shouldn't ask about it. Besides, she seemed to be trying to cover for it now. "Dale does, in a small house closer to the main road. You probably didn't see it through the forest over there."

In his side vision, he saw her flick a look over at him. She'd trailed her gaze over him a few times the day before, but he couldn't tell if she liked what she saw or not. It didn't matter, but he liked to think she did.

"Have you always been around horses?"

"My dad made his living from horses, and I always have, too." He felt his shoulders relax, though he hadn't realized before how stiff he'd been. Maybe they could manage this. "When we finish today, you might want to go check out some books on horses. I'll go over everything with you, but it'd help if you can tell a bridle from a stirrup."

"I'm not that slow."

"I'm just saying, I'd like you to know what everything is. Horse breeds, grasses, a little about horse care. Check into trail horses, since that's what we have here." He glanced over. "That is, if you're serious about this."

"I am." Her voice wasn't haughty like before, but heavy. Maybe she did see what she was getting into.

"This is Jack's farm coming up." He pulled down a long gravel drive. Ready for them, Jack waved and swung open the barn door, but he scratched his thick, gray beard as he looked at Missy. Hopping out, Brent told him, "Jack Wilson, this is Ben's sister, Missy Nelson."

"Ben had a sister?" At Jack's words, Brent gave her a look.

She narrowed her eyes as she stepped back. He knew that she wouldn't be much help. Her petite frame couldn't be more than five feet five, and the bales were stinking heavy. Still, she needed to see what they did.

Jack jumped up into the truck bed and stacked the bales as Brent loaded them. He paused after a minute to toss her a pair of gloves.

"I noticed you don't have a pair." He waited while she slipped them on. "Want to help out?"

He threw another bale into the bed to demonstrate and stepped back to let her try.

Bending, she grabbed the strings and pulled. "Holy crap!"

He couldn't stop the laugh, but he managed to keep it silent. Too bad she caught him shaking when she stood up.

"Would you like to keep the steering wheel warm?" He grinned with the comment so she'd know it was in fun.

"You jerk!" She glared. "There are other ways I can help out on the ranch."

He sobered because her eyes grew smoldering with anger. They looked amber, and entrancing. He felt his breathing quicken.

Turning, she walked to the front of the truck and got back in the passenger seat. He went back to work, shrugging at Jack's puzzled look. They both looked in the back window at her stiff shoulders and knew to keep silent as they worked.

"That about does it," Jack said when he stacked the last one.

"See you, Jack," Brent waved and joined Missy in the cab to head back. With her arms folded, she turned her body away and didn't speak the entire trip home.

This wasn't so bad, he thought with a glance her way. If they could stay angry at each other, he wouldn't have to wonder about her.

When they reached the stables, he backed his truck up to unload the hay, but he didn't get out when he turned off the engine. "Listen, I'll find you something else to do."

She nodded.

Trying not to grin again, he asked, "It was funny, wasn't it?"

Her head turned. When her gaze locked with his, the truck cab grew suddenly smaller. Talk about one determined lady.

He saw her Nez Pierce heritage in her high, proud cheekbones and skin the color of red baked clay. She had a face someone could stare at for hours.

But not him. Right?

Brent knew she had her own agenda, not a relationship, on her mind. Well, she wasn't the only one.

## Chapter Two

"So this is the reality behind the mystery," she said as she threw another shovel of dirty hay, and then watched her breath puff away in the frigid evening air. *Smelly* cold air, since it carried the smell of the animal's waste.

"What's that?" Brent's face came into view over the wall that separated the stalls they worked in. "What mystery?"

"I've just never seen cowboys in movies doing this stuff." Although, she didn't remember watching too many westerns.

"Mucking stalls is mysterious? So, what do you know about horse breeding?" He went back to work, but she saw his smile before his face disappeared.

"Stop right there. I'll stick to this for now." She liked his smile. That friendly smile shocked her. He had a cleft chin, something she liked in men, back when she was interested in them. The only thing she wanted with Brent was friendship, and a working partnership.

Working was the operative word. They'd been busy all day. Here it was evening already, and they were still cleaning horse stalls. He'd told her they wouldn't normally do this so late, but he'd spent the day showing her around.

At least they'd formed an unspoken truce and found a way to work together. His remarks weren't as cutting as when they'd first met.

She rested her shovel on the ground for a minute to rub the small of her back. All this work had almost been worth the view of him on a horse yesterday.

Tall and long and wearing his cowboy hat. She'd gawked at him from around a corner, amazed by his control and grace as he moved around the corral. She liked how he held his back straight when he rode.

"Did you read those books I suggested?" he asked while he worked. Hello reality, she chided herself.

"Yup." All that knowledge sure did help with this particular job, too.

"Ready to try riding tomorrow?"

She popped up this time to look at him. "Riding horses?"

Straightening, he turned to look at her. "No, a four-wheeler," he said with a forced serious face.

She huffed at him and finished her job, betting he smiled now that she wasn't watching him. She needed a hot shower to warm her up, a good dinner, and a good book to read.

Her body wasn't used to this kind of work, but she welcomed the experience. She also liked how busy it kept her. And boy, did he keep her busy. Not only did he work her till the daylight faded - around five o'clock thanks to old man winter - but he kept her mind busy with fantasies of what his lean body could do for her.

Not that she'd ever let that happen, but he was just too incredible. Too hot. He looked like he would know just what to do and where to do it.

*Missy!* Cool it. She needed to get out of there before she moaned at her thoughts.

"Okay, I'm done here," she said with finality in case he had some other chore in mind. Since he wasn't finished, she watched him work for a minute, expecting some kind of answer.

Good thing he wasn't interested in women, because he could seduce her if he had the right personality. Nice long legs, nice butt. She was more of a face person, and he had one great face. Long and narrow. Startling eyes in a unique blue color. She liked his sandy hair and secretive expression, too. He often got a gleam in his eyes that dared her to break him.

"Missy," he said as he set aside his shovel. He leaned against a rail to wipe his brow with the long sleeve of his shirt. "Are you settled in?"

Thinking of the messy cabin she now called home, she said, "I thought you didn't want me to stick around."

"No need for you to be uncomfortable while you're here."

"But it won't be long, right?" Shocked at herself, she took a step toward the door.

"Hey, just trying to be nice." He looked perplexed, maybe even annoyed at her. He had one eyebrow lower than the other in what she already recognized as his scowl.

"You're right. We don't need to be so mean to each other. I'm used to competing with everyone around me." She wanted to rub her sore shoulders, but she couldn't let herself in front of him. "Yes, I'm settled in some. See you tomorrow, Brent."

Touching his hat, he called, "Your first riding lesson."

She couldn't wait, she thought, but she stopped by the doors and turned. Maybe she could try acting human for a minute. "I'm sorry about Ben, that you lost a good friend."

That shouldn't have been so hard, or taken her so long, but she felt her nerves act up while he stared at her.

"Thanks, goodnight." He turned away, moving onto another task. She felt uneasy as she left, wondering how he was dealing with the loss.

The night seemed more black than any other night of her life. The ever present clouds blocked the moon and starlight, while sending the thinnest ocean mist into the air. The place was majestic, she had to give it that. Not anything like the small, dry town where she grew up in Nevada. Wouldn't Brent laugh if he knew she wasn't the city girl she looked?

She'd even caught herself slipping into the easy talk she'd worked so hard to remove from her speech. After hiding her past for so long, it baffled her that she wanted Brent to know. She didn't like him thinking she was some snob who looked down at his country lifestyle.

But why did she care?

She walked on the road back to Ben's place, thankful for the pole lights at the edge of the corral. She quickened her pace, pushing her hands down into her coat pockets.

"Missy!" She heard his footsteps crunching on the gravel as he ran toward her. She turned and waited for him to catch up. Those long legs could move, couldn't they? Her body tingled even while she cursed it.

"Is everything okay?" she asked and tried her hardest to hide her relief at seeing him. He slowed and pulled in a deep breath.

"I can't let you walk home by yourself."

So he wanted to walk her, big deal. They started off together, and she asked, "Are there cougars out here?"

"I haven't seen any this close," he said. She didn't like the uncertainty of that answer, but he didn't sound worried. "So what did you do before you came here?"

"I married old men for their money," she said with a sly smile. Ducking her head didn't hide it, even in this dim light.

"I deserved that." His voice sounded like he grinned. "But I want to know."

"Advertising. I spent three years with the same company, building my clientele list, and I was promoted twice." She'd still be there if it weren't for the lies and her ruined reputation. She thought of going back, applying at another firm in another city, but Russ, her former boss, would never give her a good reference. "My career might be over."

That hadn't been the best thing to say. He didn't ask about it, so she hoped he either hadn't heard or didn't care. They took several steps in silence. Unbearable silence, but she couldn't find her tongue to speak.

"Do you want to go back to that?" he asked softly, his head tilted. Apparently he had heard her loud and clear, and now his eyes were trained on her face.

She tried to laugh. "Yeah, yeah. You don't want me here."

"I didn't mean that, and you know it," he nudged her arm. Shrugging, she left the question unanswered.

They were about to her door when she said, "So you've been around horses all your life, but did you grow up in Oregon?"

"West Coast born and breed," he said. "I can't live without the ocean, the mountains, and streams all over the place."

"You don't mind the rain and fog?" She gestured around them.

"We do have dry summers. Nice autumns, too." He looked amused. "But I like the rain, keeps the tall trees watered."

"Don't cowboys belong in Texas?"

"Lots of people ride out here. Just wait till you get a horse down on the sand. The trails are great, too, with the view of the ocean."

Did her cold cowboy just warm up to her? Instinct almost made her jump for a smart remark, but another part of her - the bigger part - was tired of keeping up the front.

"Thanks for walking me." She paused at the door and looked at him in the porch light. He'd pushed his hands down in his jeans pockets, but pulled one free to nudge his hat back. She didn't want him to go just yet. "I've been wondering . . . What are your plans for this place?"

A sudden smile brightened his face. "I could talk on that all night. Ben and I used to talk about it while we rode over the property, about buying more horses, maybe more land later on."

His excitement dimmed. She felt his loss then, remembered at the same minute that Ben wasn't here for those future days. They nodded before she went in. Inside, she leaned against the closed door and heard his first steps as he left.

* * * *

The picture seemed off . . . she leaned against the corral rail, but the ground wasn't dusty and the sun didn't beat down on her.

Instead, tall cedars surrounded them, with graceful limbs bowing as they leaned out. Wispy clouds lay up in the sky like streaks of whipped cream while the sun warmed her skin. She smelled salt in the air, mixed with forest scents. The oddity was completed by the seagulls that called out to each other. She looked down from the birds just as Brent led Jeffery out of the stable entrance.

Brent's jeans hugged his legs all the way up. Then his shirt molded to his trim waist before stretching across his shoulders. She looked at the horse as he drew closer so he wouldn't see the way she admired every inch of him.

"I'm going to ride your horse?" Could it be a good sign? Or did he plan a big joke on her? She hated uncertainty worse than anything, and he put her on shaky ground time and time again.

"I trust him, and believe me, you'll want a horse we can trust." He motioned for her to come over. That authoritative gesture sent hot licks of want up her. The sensation shocked her senseless for a minute. He motioned again.

"Okay, okay." *Keep your senses about you, girl.* The speckled monster pawed the ground and looked her over. She joined Brent on the horse's left side.

"Offer your hand, like you did before." Brent instructed. "He senses your fear."

Fear? She wanted to argue, but she wasn't much of a liar. After she looked at Brent, she held out her hand and Jeffery rubbed his soft nose in it.

"All right, boy," Brent soothed. "This lady needs to learn how to ride, and you're just the horse to do it."

After he reassured the horse, he turned to her. "I'm putting you on the fast track to riding. We could put you up there bareback so you could learn to lead, but you said you're fast learner, right?"

Was that a dare? "I am."

"We'll get you up there, then you can get used to how it feels. Next you'll practice leading him with the reins. Now watch." He grabbed the saddle, put his foot in the stirrup, and swung up. After he dismounted, he nodded for her to try.

Just like that, huh?

"Hand here." He took her hand and pulled it up. She jumped at his touch. A small jump, but she felt it all the way through her.

His hat threw shade over his eyes, but she was pretty sure he'd seen.

"Foot there," he said. She nodded and pretended not to hear the amusement just begging to slip through his steady voice. She did as instructed and placed her foot in the stirrup.

"Up and at 'em." He swatted her bottom as she started up.

"Ahh!" Her foot came back down hard, and she spun around to stare at him, open-mouthed. No other man had ever made her body tingle like this. Did she feel frustration or heat for him?

"Sorry, ma'am, just messing around." His dazzling smile faded into a remorseful grin. She licked her lips and tried to make it look like an angry gesture. Brows scrunched, she placed her hands again and tried to do what he'd shown her. She made it halfway up before the thought of him behind her, so close, sent her right back down.

"Darn it!" Not only did Brent laugh, but his men joined in from their spot by the fence. She hadn't been aware they watched her.

"Ignore them." Brent rested an arm against the horse, then rested his forehead against his arm. He couldn't be fed up with her already, she worried, before gritting her teeth and waiting.

"Let's just breathe."

Did he say breathe? She crossed her arms, but he straightened up and grabbed her wrists, pulling them to her sides. He'd trapped her so she had to look at him. Even with the shade on his eyes, she could see their cool blue color and knowing look.

"Just like that, Missy. Now close your eyes."

"What?"

"Close them."

They snapped shut. Knowing he was inches from her face, watching her, made her breathe faster and faster. She couldn't hear anything but the air she sucked in.

"I want you to stay just like that until you calm down." His hands softly squeezed her arms. She could do this, she could! Sounds of the countryside became louder as her breathing became quiet. But his strong, quiet voice still sounded in her head.

She never liked it when men told her what to do, so she didn't understand the pleasant chills his commands sent through her.

Also surprising was the comfort she felt from his hands on her.

"Calm now?" His voice sounded so near. Close enough to tilt her mouth up and kiss him. No, no, no! Breathe.

She nodded to his question after several deep breaths.

"Good, now open your eyes and try again." He let go and stepped back, ending the closeness.

Now steady, she felt riled for reacting to him that way. But she was back in her game.

"Once more, and that's it?" She poured on the sugar with that one, just to let him know she wouldn't fall prey to his charm. He raised an eyebrow at her, like he was questioning her cockiness.

"You sure you're cut out for this?" His teasing tone was back as he watched. She swung up and made it this time.

After the men whooped, she said, "I'm glad I'm at least giving you some entertainment."

Jeffery snorted, but remained still. She became fully aware now that she had a live animal under her, one that had a mind of his own.

"Yup, now you're in the saddle," Brent said from below. "Do you know what to do up there?"

"What?" Her concentration went to crap. Jeffery decided to show her what to do and started moving slowly around in a circle.

"Grab the reins!" One of the men yelled from the fence.

"I got it." She declared to all three men and the horse. "I watched you guys do it, I read how to do it, and now I'm going to do it."

"All right, Missy, do you know how to lead him?" Brent prompted her and then watched.

"Pull in the direction I want to go, right?"

"Hope you kept your job back home," he joked.

"I lost it before the lawyer called me." She spoke, but kept her mind on her task this time. "The jackass I worked for sent me packing when I thought we should cool things." Her hands gripped the reins like she was hanging over a cliff, but the horse finally let her lead. She risked a quick glance over at Brent to grin in victory. "Why are you looking at me like that?"

He looked displeased about something.

"You slept with your boss?"

"Huh?" Her horse took the opportunity to jerk her the other way. She had to twist her head sharply to look at Brent. "What are you talking about?"

"What you just said. He fired you over it."

"That's not what I said!" She jerked the reins and the horse made an angry noise. Oh, crap. Jeffery jerked upward again.

Heart flying up her throat, she bit off a scream.

"Calm now!" Brent called in a mellow voice. She remembered, from her reading, to lean forward to keep on top of the monster.

She sucked in air like she was drowning. Since she had to keep both hands on the reins, she couldn't rub her chest like she wanted. Brent's laughter sang out, startling her almost as much as the horse had.

When he was serious again, he said, "Calm down, take him around."

On her first trip around, he walked a few steps from the horse. If he was nervous about her riding Jeffery, it didn't show. Thankful for his calmness, she felt herself relax. They came along side the two men who still watched.

"Howdy, ma'am," one said, touching his hat.

"That's Dale," Brent introduced him, "And the tall one's Ivan."

She glanced over and nodded, but that was all she could do at the moment.

Brent told the men, "You two should be working, not gawking."

Jeffery moved away so she didn't hear their responses. With the sun shining brighter than before, she grew warm. This was work, but it wasn't as bad as she imagined. She'd dreamed the night before that she fell off while Brent watched. So far, so good.

She rode Jeffery around again. As she approached Brent, he told her to stop the horse.

"Huh?" Yeah, he was being mean. She tugged on the reins, but as gently as she could. She didn't want to tick the horse off again.

Jeffery stopped.

Brent, next to them, nudged back his hat to look up at her. She gave him a sweet smile. "That wasn't hard."

"You're done?"

That was a trick question, but she did want back down on the ground.

"Yeah, I want down from here. Are you going to help me?"

A smile tugged on his lips. What else could she do? She'd rather ask for help than land on her butt trying to get off by herself.

"You want my help?" he asked as he held her gaze. "That means I'll have to touch you."

The word 'touch' rolled off his tongue as if he'd said 'caress'. She knew he teased about her reaction to his rear swatting, but she wouldn't react this time around.

She asked, "Afraid of my cooties?"

She made light of his comment, but her body was on a completely different wave length as she thought about his hands on her. *Listen up*, she thought to herself, *he's a man, just a regular guy working a ranch*. A regular guy with a sexy, quick grin, and a voice that could soothe her rattled nerves back from the edge.

"Grab the horn and swing your leg back over." He stepped close, ready to ease her down. She gripped the pommel and pulled her leg over. Just then he pressed his hand against her hip. "Easy now."

That was not - *was not!* - the place to touch a woman while telling her to take it easy. She felt her traitorous body jerk and could only pray he didn't notice.

She slid against him the entire way down, and fell back into his chest. He hadn't moved, so she couldn't either. Her heartbeat jack hammered into overdrive as her back pressed into him.

Could be worse.

Could be her *front* pressed into him.

"I . . . I, ah, need a bath." *I need out of here!* His arms encircled her and she couldn't look away from his bare forearms. Lightly tanned. Strong.

"A bath?" he asked as if he'd been thinking about it.

She recognized the bedroom voice. "I've never been on a horse before. It tends to make a person sore."

He eased back, holding the reins still, and gave her room to step away.

"Would you like to see how to take the tack off and cool down the horse before you go?" he asked with a hand on her shoulder to guide her back a step.

"Sure." She walked beside him into the stable yard, glad for the space between them. This touching didn't mean anything. At least it shouldn't.

She didn't say much while she helped him, but her mind ran around in self-defeating circles.

How could she have accidentally mentioned Russ and what happened at her old job? After that, Brent had turned on the charm. Now he thought she was easy.

"Well, that was fun." She nodded and marched outside like she had important things to do.

\* \* \* \*

She didn't do bad at all in the end, he thought as he watched her go. So why did she turn into a stiff greenhorn when he brought Jeffery out? He wouldn't have thought he could make her nervous . . . or that he could calm her down like that.

He'd gotten an aching erection while he watched her breathe with her eyes closed. As far as he could tell, no one saw. Boy, he'd never hear the end of it.

"That little lady's got you already." Dale's voice boomed from behind him. Brent turned, giving the robust man a hard look.

"I can't send her away." He yanked his gloves off and stuffed them into his jean pocket. "I explained it to you."

"You said she'd be helping out around here. Looks like she don't know a lick about horses."

*A Cowboy For Christmas*

Dale shook his head like this was one of the worse offenses committable.

"She's learning fast." Was he defending her?

"What about our work?" Dale pressed.

"Hey, I'll handle it." After a pause, Brent added, "I saw you and Ivan watching her today."

"Yeah, you aren't the only one." Dale seemed to think it was funny. He had a mustache, black like his hair, and he always had a half smile on his face.

It wasn't that he wanted her, Brent just didn't want anyone saying something suggestive about Missy. "Listen, you're right about how much work we have to do around here."

"So leave the drooling to you?"

"This isn't funny." At least, only in a really irritating way. "I'm not drooling over her. I'm showing her what we do around here so she'll see she isn't cut out for it."

"Oh." Dale gave him a conspiracy-style nod before going into a good belly laugh. Brent turned and strode away, straight for Ben's house.

But it was Missy's house now. Everything felt out of whack with Ben gone. With Missy around. No joking with Ben, riding together, talking about next year and their dreams for their ranch.

How was he supposed to feel about the woman?

He banged on her door twice and waited, but she didn't answer. He knew she'd gone inside, so he cracked it and called her name.

A muffled noise came back. Irritation made him itch all over as he wavered at the door.

Cursing himself, he quietly walked across the front room to the hallway. She'd made a good dent in the mess, he saw, by stacking boxes and papers in the corner. "Missy?"

"Brent?" she called from the bathroom. He heard either surprise or panic in her voice. "Do you mind? I'm taking a bath."

"Oh," he tried to remember why he came. "I need to talk to you."

"Now?" She sighed. "Well, you're here. Start talking."

"For a city girl, you don't have much class." That didn't sound as funny out loud as it had in his head.

"I've got a surprise for you, cowboy. I grew up in a small dirt town."

She did? She didn't look like it, though she didn't exactly talk like city dweller, either. "My men spent all day watching you instead of working."

"So talk to them, not me."

He opened his mouth, an argument in mind, but just then his mind came up with a picture of Missy on the other side of the door . . . in the bathtub . . . surrounded by pretty pink bubbles. A nice hot bath sounded pretty darn tempting at the moment.

"Are you still there?" she asked through the door.

"Uh, sorry. I was thinking about what I'd say to Dale and Ivan."

"Hmm, I bet."

Now what? He tried to think up a comeback, but what could he say to a naked woman in the tub? *Can I join you?* He spun around and headed out.

# Chapter Three

The darkness, the cold, but mostly the quiet didn't make for a good evening as Brent stood with Dale outside the stables. He thought about inviting him up to the house, but while he thought about it, Dale excused himself to go home. He wanted to see his girl, Alice.

Brent couldn't remember the last time he was alone and actually felt alone. He sighed and walked through the stables to say goodnight to the horses. Missy hadn't asked which ones had been Ben's, meaning they were hers now. Seemed odd to him. If she wanted money, she could sell them. He didn't like that thought one bit.

Dancer snorted at him, like he was asking where Ben had gone.

"Sorry, buddy." *Sorry Ben's not here.* He faced forward, and though he wanted to turn and look at the stallion, he couldn't.

Shaking his head, he left. How had he gotten so spooked about the whole thing? The horse couldn't blame him. No one did. So why did he feel so guilty about Ben?

Outside again, he headed for his house, but he spotted Missy walking on the road, bundled up in her red coat and a scarf. Guess the cougar comment hadn't scared her enough to keep her inside after dark.

"Want company?" he called out because she looked lonely. How could she not be when she'd left her life to come out here? It looked like she shrugged, so he jogged over. "What are you doing out here by yourself? It's late."

"It's seven in the evening." She rubbed her nose in the cold.

"And cold."

"You're out here, too." She blew out a breath. If she hadn't run earlier, he might have asked her to go into town for a movie or dinner.

"Did you eat dinner yet?" Where had that come from? That was worse than inviting her into town. One look at her expression in the yard light confirmed that she was not going anywhere alone with him. He spared them both. "Guess not. Are you heading back?"

"Yes, want to walk me again?" They turned together. He spotted mud on her boots. She hadn't balked at hard work or getting dirty. Maybe she'd done this before.

"So you didn't grow up in a city?" He remembered her expensive suit, the glitter on her ears and fingers, and the perfume that made him want to lean in closer to sniff.

With a laugh, she asked, "You don't believe me?"

"Tell me about it." The fancy clothes and jewelry were gone, but she still smelled like that perfume. It was a light smell that seemed to evade him. He got whiffs of it here and there.

"Not much to tell, really. My dad owned cattle, but we didn't live on a ranch."

He could tell her mind was going off somewhere.

"Did you want to?" Could that be what she was sad about? He knew so little about her.

"No, not at all. I wanted to go somewhere bigger and better. So I went off to the closest city at the first chance I got."

Maybe that's where things went wrong. He was sure something had somewhere along the line, but he didn't know how to ask her about it.

She looked at the ground like she was ignoring him, but she started talking. "I think that's why our father left his money to Ben."

"Whoa, because you didn't want to live on a cattle ranch?" he asked, hearing the hurt in her voice. A picture of her came to mind, when she came to his house the first time, and looked so hurt and lost.

"Ben chose a more traditional lifestyle, and our father was proud of his Nez Pierce heritage." She shook her head as if she wanted to end the conversation. But she added, "I didn't mean to insult that, I just wanted excitement. I was raised as an only child, and it was quiet. All the time."

Hearing this made him want to reach out to her, but again, his instincts told him she'd freeze up on him if he did. "Most young people do." And she did look young, maybe twenty-five. Her age didn't agree with the hurt he saw in her eyes sometimes.

"That's why I didn't come here sooner . . . to see Ben." She rubbed her nose again to warm it up, but she still didn't look at him. "Our father left everything to Ben. I didn't even know about him until Dad died. I didn't want to know him at first."

They reached her house and she stepped up, turning to say goodbye.

"Missy, I got the wrong impression of you." He didn't like saying he was wrong, but he figured that came pretty darn close.

"Thanks, I think." She tried for a laugh and turned. He didn't want this to end and grabbed for something to keep her talking.

"What about your job? What happened there?"

She glanced back while keeping her hand on the door handle. "Listen, I appreciate your interest, or concern if that's what it is, but there's certain things I can't share with you. Goodnight."

The door shut before he could answer. Yeah, things went wrong for her, and it had to be her job, and the boss she'd mentioned. Russ.

Turning, he started back. So they both had their secrets.

\* \* \* \*

She left the cabin when the morning light was strong enough to see. Brent hadn't mentioned what time he started in the morning, but she usually found him working when she headed down to the stables.

Though he'd never admit to it, she felt certain he was taking it easy on her, and that was both endearing and disappointing. When she said she wanted to prove herself, she meant it.

The high, thin cloud cover cracked here and there, showing off stretches of innocent blue. She couldn't ignore the sweet scent in the air or the bright colors all around, from the thick green grass to the array of oranges in the autumn oak leaves. A squirrel stopped on the road ahead of her and clicked as she approached.

The road took her past Brent's house on the way to the stables. She looked over when a door

*A Cowboy For Christmas*

shut. Brent jogged down the stairs and came her way, wearing a bulky green coat that hid his torso, but his jeans didn't hide anything about his legs.

He touched his hat when he reached her. "Morning, Missy. You're up early."

She got a shiver when he said her name, but she blamed it on the cold. "Yeah, I'd thought I'd come by and try to catch you in the shower." She hoped for his grin and wasn't disappointed. It wouldn't bother her to spend some time appreciating his easy style and charm while she was here. Nothing wrong with that, right? As long as he didn't show any interest in her, or in taking advantage of her, she liked this setup.

"What gross or painful chores do you have planned for today?" She thought about the first time she'd seen him. At least they weren't enemies now. Friends? With the hormones zinging between them, she wasn't sure they could ever be friends, but a truce was nice.

"I'm going to check the paths and fences. Thought you said you're ready to take a horse out of the corral."

"How could I be ready?" One riding lesson and he thought she could ride a horse? He looked like he enjoyed watching her expression, so she sucked it up. "Sure, why not?"

"Don't worry. I'm good at teaching. It's part of what we do out here, remember?"

She kept a good two feet between them as they walked. They had flirted and eyed each other the past few days, but she wanted to put a stop to it. If they got involved, how would she get a fair chance here? How would she trust him?

He glanced over several times. She bet her thoughts were written all over her face, but that was a good thing, at least this time. He needed to know how things were between them.

"How long are you planning on keeping that rental?" He asked as they neared the stables.

"I need a vehicle." She needed something to remind her she could leave if she chose, and that she was here by her own decision.

"There's a pickup we keep around. Why don't I give you keys to it?"

She met his eyes, uncertain of his intentions. It would save her money, at a time when she didn't have it coming in. Still, she said, "I don't know."

"I hadn't thought about it, but Ben paid cash for it last year. Just a little truck, about fifteen years old, but it runs. Suppose it's yours."

Uncomfortable, she tightened her scarf and thought it over.

"I guess . . . Then I can take the rental back and not worry about it anymore." She didn't like how awkward it felt at times, to use Ben's things. Did it bother Brent? When she looked back at him, he met her gaze, probably seeing her doubt.

"It's just the way it is. I was pissy when you got here, but it wasn't about you. Believe me."

Unable to answer with words, she nodded. At the stables, he took her around to the tack room. "We keep the keys right here. Here's an extra set."

He dropped them in her hand. *Thank you* stuck in her throat. Just a few days ago, he had wanted to run her off. Now he handed her keys to one of the ranch vehicles.

He watched her face, so she nodded like it wasn't that big of a deal.

"You can take Speckle today. She's gentle and isn't particular about who rides her." He pulled equipment down for them to use.

"Speckle?"

"She's an Appaloosa like Jeffery, and she came with the name. She's your horse, now, guess you can rename her. But she might not like it." He waited for her to lead the way into the stables. She noted he'd grabbed one saddle. "Pad first."

Since he held it out to her, she assumed she was going to learn how to saddle a horse. So she laid the blanket over the horse's back. The black horse, across the way, watched and protested loudly. Missy gave Brent a look since she didn't get horse talk yet.

"He wants to go, but I'm not taking him out with you along." He didn't elaborate on why, but Missy turned to the angry beast, remembering it had been Ben's horse.

"What's his name again?"

"Dancer." He flicked a look back at the horse and turned back. She hadn't seen him pay attention to Dancer at all, now that she thought about it.

"He misses Ben," she said, wanting to sooth the horse but didn't dare reach out to him. Brent waited with the saddle, so she went to work.

Judging by the look in Brent's eyes and the emotional charge to the air, he missed Ben too, but she wouldn't say that now.

She heaved the saddle up and adjusted it. A book she'd checked out had shown her how to lace up the girth strap and cinch it. Though he didn't direct her, she gave it a try.

"Hook the stirrup," he said, pointing.

"That's it?" she asked, looking it over. Should she ask him to check it?

"Looks good," he said as he tugged on it here and there. "Lead her out. I'll saddle Jeffery."

Outside, she made it up on the first try. It was easier without Brent standing behind her where he could stare at her bottom.

"Hey, Speckle," she said to the horse and rubbed her neck to get acquainted. They needed to trust each other. Trust wasn't something she gave away easily, but this felt different.

Brent emerged with Jeffery.

"Hey, look at me. First try, even." She couldn't remember the last time she felt gleeful. She breathed in the cold air, feeling snappy and alive.

"I am looking." He mounted his horse and clicked. She almost missed his comment, but suddenly did a double take at him.

She started to say something about it, but she did ask for it, didn't she? One side of his mouth lifted, and he moved his horse up next to hers.

"Speckle knows what she's doing," Brent said, tilting his head to look at her, "So you'll be getting used to sitting up there on the trials."

They rode out along the pasture and then turned into the forest of cedar and pine. Brent glanced over every few minutes, but he never commented. She hoped that meant she was doing okay. Ferns grew in clumps on the ground under the forest canopy. Water dripped off everything.

"Feel okay?"

"I love it." She didn't want to look so happy in front of him, but when he gave her an honest, friendly smile, she couldn't hold it in.

"I thought all this would be hard for you." He ducked under a pine branch. "You sure you've never done this before?"

She shook her head.

"Missy?" he persisted.

"All right. I wanted to ride when I was younger."

"Your father wouldn't let you?"

"They used four wheelers. And feedlots. I couldn't stand to see the cattle in their pens. It seemed like they were always slaughtering." She stopped and turned her face away. She didn't care how friendly they got, she wasn't going to cry in front of him.

"Sounds like it's a good thing this is a horse ranch."

They rode in silence until they reached the top of a hill, where she could see the ocean far below, rolling in wave after white wave. She'd never smelled the ocean before, and could only describe it as a salty deep sea smell.

The water jetted up where it hit giant boulders. Cold. Dangerous. And breathtaking. Since he let her sit for several minutes to just gaze out, she forgot that he watched her.

The water stretched endless to the north and south while it faded into the sky in front of them. She couldn't distinguish the line where ocean and sky met.

"Now do you see why I love Oregon?" Brent's soft voice drifted into her thoughts like the waves moving inland below.

Turning, she hoped her expression worked for an answer. Something so vast, mysterious, and alive left her without words for it.

So did Brent. He looked magnificent with the pale blue sky behind him and his blue eyes reflecting all the color around them. He sat with such ease, but his eyes weren't relaxed. They were fixated on her like the wind might steal her away.

Well, she gawked right back, so she couldn't sass him about it.

"I've never seen the ocean this way." Her whisper mixed with the singing breeze and the soft, subtle ocean music. "Just from an airplane. This is much better."

"I'd have to agree." He held her still with his gaze. Just then the breeze brought his scent to her nose. Man, hay, and something refreshing. Her hair whipped across her face, and she joined reality with a jerk.

Something was brewing . . . weather-wise.

"Well, we got half a day of clear skies." Brent still didn't look away and now she burned all over. "Guess we oughta get back before you get soaked." The corners of his mouth twitched.

"Yeah, I'd need another long, hot bath." She turned just before she smiled.

\* \* \* \*

"Brent?"

He heard her call from the stable entrance. His hands paused as he filed Dancer's hoof, but he fought the desire to look up at Missy.

He waved instead of calling back since the horse was a bit jumpy. Dale and Ivan had held off on taking care of Dancer until he could get there. All three of them were wary of the horse. It missed Ben something mighty.

"Sounds like she's done brushing Speckle already." Dale jabbed him. "You can go on with her."

"I started this." Brent kept working, knowing Missy would come over to talk to them. "Ivan, don't let her get too close to him."

He glanced up to see her, but then he couldn't get his attention back on the job at hand.

She stood by the corner to look for him as she gathered her hair over one shoulder. Her petite body looked delicate, but her eyes said right away not to mess with her. As he watched, she stuffed her hands in her pockets and started his way.

The horse partially hid him, so maybe she wouldn't see him stare. Her green sweater did something to her skin, made it richer in color. He thought of her almond brown eyes watching him as she sat on her horse. Whatever was happening between them . . . well, it couldn't be good if it consumed his mind every second of the day.

Dancer snorted, so he made a soothing sound as he watched her.

"Brent!" Dale jerked toward him.

"Uhh!" His yell was cut short as he hit the ground. Pain sparked in his ribs, blocking out the pain of impact with the ground. Damn horse kicked him!

He looked up at clouds, cursing his hormones, cursing Missy, the horse, and his damn wondering eyes.

He saw Dale and Ivan lean over him. "That's one quick horse." Ivan added a few swear words as he looked at the horse and then Brent.

"Ivan get the horse back!" Dale ordered and knelt down. "Brent?"

He held a hand out so Dale wouldn't touch him. He didn't need fussing over, no matter how many ribs he'd broken. His side throbbed, but he couldn't get a breath in to say so.

"Brent?"

At her voice, Dale laughed. Brent tried for an evil glare directed at Dale as Missy came close enough to see Brent on the ground.

She looked so genuinely worried Brent wanted to smile, if he didn't hurt so darn bad.

"Holy crap! What happened?"

"Not crap, ma'am. The horse kicked him." Dale held eye contact with Brent and rubbed his chin, a nervous habit. "He wasn't ready."

"Yeah," Ivan joined in. "His mind must have been elsewhere."

Brent made a mental list of everything he'd say to them as soon as he could talk.

"Aren't you going to help him up?" She knelt beside him.

"Maybe we shouldn't move him just yet." Dale, at last, sounded worried.

Brent didn't want all of them to worry over him, so he forced himself up onto his elbows. This time he couldn't hide the pain.

"It's your side, isn't it?" Dale didn't wait for the answer, but braced Brent against him, pulled him to his feet, and started for the truck.

"Do you want me to come along?" Missy offered, her hands clasped in front of her. He wanted to reassure her, but he sure as heck didn't want her at the hospital with him.

He waited until Dale got him in the truck before he looked back. Ivan was taking Dancer to the pasture. Missy hadn't moved, and still watched as they drove away.

"Gets you fast, doesn't it?" Dale asked as he steered around a corner.

Brent thought he meant the horse at first, until he looked over. Dale met his gaze with knowing eyes.

"Yup, took three days for Alice to get me."

Damn his side. He wanted to argue the point, but instead he leaned his head back and closed his eyes. Maybe the pain was good. He could think about it instead of Missy.

\* \* \* \*

They'd been gone all evening. She paced a while and then cleaned like crazy. Fractured ribs couldn't be that bad. Maybe it was a few, or maybe nothing was broken. She didn't know yet.

After a huge sigh, she started dinner. The least she could do was have something ready for him to eat. They'd been gone four hours when she walked to his house to leave dinner in his fridge.

She was glad that he didn't lock his front door. Of course, the horses didn't need to break in and steal anything.

She put his dinner away and couldn't help but think of the first time she'd stood in his kitchen. How had so much changed so fast?

Slowly, she walked into the other room. She'd clean for him, but he kept the place spotless. Should she call the hospital? That'd make him happy. She again noticed how bare the house looked. It needed a few small paintings, decorative rugs, something. She shook her head at herself and left.

Back in her house, she tried to finish a book but couldn't. At eight, she went outside, thinking she'd missed the truck.

The cold knocked her back inside, so she got her coat and stepped out again.

A clear night. That didn't happen too often. The stars were suspended in layers, some close and some distant. She stared up for a minute and listened to the night. A dove cooed several times as it settled in for the night.

Did Ivan take care of the horses? Things were messed up tonight, so she'd check. Brent's house was still dark when she walked by.

The horses were in their stalls, but they didn't have blankets on them.

"Let's hope I do this right. No laughing," she told them as she pulled a blanket over the first horse. It looked like a coat to her, with Velcro in the front to secure it, but Brent had called it a blanket. Course he'd used the same word for the smaller blanket that went under the saddle.

She didn't worry about getting in the stall with Jeffery, Speckle, or the other horses. But Dancer watched her with knowing eyes.

"Hey, there." She could feel each beat of her heart. "Don't kick me, too, okay?"

She didn't get behind him. From the railing, she leaned and draped the blanket around him.

His noises sounded sad. She stepped back and reached out with one hand. What had happened today?

When he nuzzled her hand, she got the impression he knew who she was. Her heart grew heavy, the same way it had when she'd first slept in Ben's old house.

"I'm Missy," she said, surprised that she didn't feel strange for talking to a horse.

Dancer snorted. The truck rumbled softly and grew louder. She patted him goodbye and went to

*A Cowboy For Christmas*

the entrance to watch Dale pull up and help Brent out. She waited until Dale left before walking over.

She pulled her coat closer and rubbed her nose. If she wanted to stay, she'd have to get used to the weather at some point.

At Brent's door, she knocked and went in. He couldn't get up and come to the door, after all. Dale had left the hallway light on, and it shone into Brent's room.

She sucked in a breath when she saw him with his eyes closed in sleep. He'd rolled his head a little to one side, and the light fell on him. She hadn't noticed his thick eyelashes before, or how full and pouty his mouth looked. Add that to his movie-star cleft chin, and he had one handsome face.

What would it feel like to cradle his face in her hand? He didn't seem to have five o'clock shadow, but the light wasn't bright enough to tell.

His blanket was pulled up to mid chest, leaving his bare shoulders exposed. They were as nice as she'd suspected. She'd like to run her hand down his neck to his shoulder and feel his muscles. His hands lay on his stomach as it rose and fell.

She knew she shouldn't, but she started toward his bed. He looked unguarded, defenseless. Sweet and sexy.

Was she high on fresh country air? Something had taken a hold of her since she came here. It couldn't be this man.

The floor creaked when she reached his bed. His eyes opened and blinked at her. "Missy?"

She blinked back for a second. "Thought I'd check on you." Blushing, she hoped he wouldn't ask why she'd snuck into his bedroom. "How bad is it?"

His injury didn't hurt his appeal. She put her hands in her pockets, shifted her weight. *Hmm, interesting floor, isn't it?*

"I'm on bed rest for a month." His voice was quiet and low. "I think you're going to be busy."

At that comment, she looked back to his face. There wasn't the normal lift in his voice or gleam in his eyes to belie his seriousness. But he couldn't mean it, could he?

She looked him over for a long minute. "A month? I don't believe a horse could put you in bed that long."

He gave it up and smiled. "A week maybe. Just some bruised ribs."

"That's a relief." She sat down on the edge, thought about jumping up, but tried to act like she didn't feel awkward sitting there.

"Is it?" he asked, his hand sliding down and brushing hers.

"You brute!" She considered the best way to get her hands around his neck, but she settled for a soft nudge to his chest. She just couldn't punch a man while he was down. "You've thought the worst of me since I arrived."

"And you of me, haven't you?"

She crossed her arms, glancing off to the side in a big show. A guitar case leaned against the wall in the shadows.

"You play?" The case was too small for a guitar. "What is it, a banjo?"

"A violin, you snob." He wrapped an arm across himself when he laughed. Knowing he was in pain ruined her show of indignation.

"You know, you're beautiful when you laugh . . . or get shy . . . or try to ride a horse and find yourself out of control." His fingers grazed the back of her hand again. Suddenly she had no trouble calming down.

"Brent, don't . . ." She suspected he was teasing again, but she didn't want him to tease her along those lines. "Listen, if you're after someone to take care of you, I'll help. You don't have to flatter me with whatever that was."

He pulled his hand away, with a smile on his face that baffled her. He looked both sad and intrigued, like she'd just given him a difficult problem to solve. Well, she wasn't his algebra homework.

"Can you eat with that injury?" she asked before telling him what she'd brought for dinner.

"Maybe a little." He watched her too closely and she needed to get out of there. So she left for the soup she'd brought him.

When she brought it back, and he saw what it was, he asked, "Are you going to feed me?"

That sincere voice and innocent eyes almost had her. "I don't think so."

She did help him up and adjusted his pillows for him. He still watched her, and those intense eyes of his were getting to her. The mood struck her then: the dim lighting, his shirtless body, his bedroom.

"I should let you rest." She stepped back.

"I'll be getting plenty of rest this week. Stay."

She shook her head. "Sorry, it's been a long day. Goodnight." She managed not to run on her way out.

\* \* \* \*

She'd show him! That was her first thought when her eyes opened in the morning. Before the sun rose, she showered, ate breakfast, and bundled up in a sweater and raincoat.

Outside, a soft, soaking rain fell. Brent would classify it as a drizzle, but nothing would stop her from taking care of things today and the next few days while he recovered.

She hurried to meet Dale and Ivan by the stables. "So what's on for today?" She didn't react to their unbelieving looks.

Dale shrugged. "Ready to saddle up?"

In the tact room, she gathered up everything Brent had, but it took her a couple of trips to carry it all . Speckle bent an ear at her.

"I know what I'm doing," she told Speckle. She did, but she had Dale check it before she mounted. It'd be rather embarrassing, and dangerous, if it weren't done right. She also didn't want to hurt the horse.

She worked with Speckle until noon, when she wanted to take lunch to Brent. On the walk back to her house, her body let her know she'd need some time to get used to the saddle. But it was worth it, wasn't it? The gait of the horse, the breeze blowing in her hair, and the sense of freedom pulled her in.

She'd stolen Brent's crock-pot the day before, laughing all the way home that he had one. Now it sat with a hot lunch simmering in it.

It didn't smell too bad, she decided on the walk to his house. No one would call her a great cook, but she could make something edible.

She raised her hand to knock when she saw him through the window in his recliner. He was kicked back in front of the TV, a blanket lying on his legs. His ribs were wrapped, she guessed for support.

No matter how hard she tried, she couldn't get her eyes off his chest, covered in light hair. Nice pecs. Well toned arms, too.

She glanced at his face and noted, happily, he was eyeing the crock-pot and not her. Maybe he hadn't noticed her appreciating his body.

Once inside, she said, "Yeah, I took it so I could cook you lunch."

"Smells great, is it poisoned?" He was joking this time, and she was glad to see the twinkle back in his eye. Then there was another type of gleam as he took her in. His eyes met hers and she couldn't ignore the change in them.

She turned away from his gaze and went in the kitchen to get a bowl. "Do you like chicken? It's not five-star restaurant quality, but it works." She spoke just to fill the silence and break the mood.

"I don't know a man who turns down food." His words weren't laced with double meaning, but his tone sounded too heavy for the conversation.

Medication. Of course, he was taking something for the pain. Or maybe he'd gotten the idea he could scare her off this way. No matter what he was thinking, he'd changed from dislike to flirtatious so quickly that it couldn't be anything but show.

"Here you go." She brought him a tray, but managed to avoid eye contact as she placed everything for him. When she stood, she glanced at him, and he didn't look happy about the emotions he saw on her face.

"You won't join me?" he asked, but he sounded like he already knew the answer.

~ 53 ~

"There's still a lot of work to do." The excuse slipped right out. "I mean, there always is, even if you can help. You know that."

He watched her go, his eyes labeling her a wimp. She had work to do, she told herself again.

# Chapter Four

Two days later, Missy stood on Brent's porch, a bag full of sandwiches in hand, preparing herself to see him. They'd all listened to him grumble about his restrictions. Today wouldn't be any different.

The door opened, ending any buffer she'd hoped for. "Hey there." He'd pulled on a light blue shirt, but it wasn't buttoned.

She finally understood the pull of a man in an open shirt. He leaned into the doorframe while she stood there, trying to remember why she'd come. When she looked back at his face, he was grinning at her.

"I brought you sandwiches." She held up the bag.

"I can make my own food now, you know. I think you just like to see me . . . half naked."

"No." She shrugged. "Just being neighborly." Since coming to the ranch, she hadn't been able to resist all the little phrases they used. Nodding toward the inside, he swung open the door and led the way into the kitchen.

"So stay and eat with me. To be neighborly." He pulled out two chairs instead of waiting for an answer.

She pulled sandwiches out and said, "I took back the rental this morning."

"About time."

"I would have kept it, but you keep thinking I'm going to run off."

"Women tend to." He took a hefty bite of his lunch and raised an eyebrow at her.

*Women tend to?* Not all women, she wanted to argue, but apparently some woman had run off on him.

She didn't want to fight with him today, plus she had a mouth full of food. A radio on the counter played music from a country station. He tapped his foot while staring out the window, lost in the music.

She wanted his shirt buttoned but could only imagine the teasing she'd endure if she asked him. Instead she pretended not to notice his well-defined muscles. Besides, she could stare at his blue eyes or his lips while he chewed.

"So, Brent, do you actually cook in your crock pot?" She tried her best to ask with a straight face.

"I don't have it just to look at."

"You do?" What if he could cook, *really* cook, and he'd been choking down her food? Meeting his gaze, she shook her head at him in amusement. Somehow the man could chew and grin, *and* look sexy all at the same time. He let the opportunity to tease her pass, except for the cocky grin.

"I talked to Dale about doing some light work." He changed the subject. "Seems the three of you are pretty determined to keep me out of things."

"For your own good," she reminded. He had a different set to his face than she was used to seeing. Anger? An unpleasant flutter churned her stomach. Why would she care if he were mad at her?

"I see how it is," Brent said.

His words repeated in her head, but in another man's voice. Brent's joking tone changed into ice-cold rage. She jumped up, surprised at the vivid memory and the intense fear that came with it. For a terrifying second, she was in her old office.

"Missy?" Brent materialized in front of her, his voice soft and soothing. "What did I say?"

His eyes held confusion as he reached out and gently took her arm. She pulled free and stepped back.

"Sorry." She grabbed her jacket and hurried out. There were reasons why she couldn't trust a man, she reminded herself. She wouldn't hide from every male on the planet, but that didn't mean she should let her guard down, either.

Shaking the memory out of her head, she picked up her pace and headed toward the stables though she didn't have a plan.
When she walked by the pasture, Dancer trotted up to the fence and whinnied at her.

"Well, hey." She walked over, holding her hand out and talking to him. His size had scared her before, but he smelled her hand. "I know I'm not Ben, but I'd like to be friends."

As if agreeing, Dancer bobbed his head before turning and putting on a show for her. Running and bucking, he whipped around the pasture in circles. Then he slowed his pace and returned to the fence.

"I see how you earned your name." He was a thing of beauty, she couldn't deny that, but she was afraid of trusting him enough to ride him. Sometime, though, someone needed to. And it didn't seem like Brent planned on it.

\* \* \* \*

"Hey, Missy!"

She jumped a foot off the ground at Brent's yell. He stood on his porch, waving at her.

What could he want? Sore from working so hard, she didn't think she could go head to head with him. He yelled again. With a sigh, she started up his walk and then the porch.

"Looking tired, city girl. How about a good home-cooked meal?"

Yeah, he'd make a nice meal, for the eyes anyway. She'd seen him in shirts and jeans, but now he wore a green T-shirt, nice and snug to show off those muscles, and sweats. They hung low on his hips and looked just too easy to pull off.

"I meant actual food, sweetie." He crossed his arms land leaned against the house. "But I can change my plans."

Did he just call her sweetie? Looking up, she saw his lips lifted more on one side, completing his come-hither look.

Pour it on, cowboy. "I'm too hungry to think like that."

Giving her a sorrowful shake of his head, he reached over and opened the front door for her to go inside. Warm air swelled out, carrying the smell of bread. She had to stop inside and breathe it in. Right behind her, he shut the door before he laughed at the incredulous look she gave him.

"Come sit down, it's ready."

She washed her hands instead, and could only hope she didn't look like she'd spent the day

*A Cowboy For Christmas*

working her butt off. Too bad she had. Maybe the smell of sweat turned him on.

"Hope you like steak," he said.

"Sure." No, she didn't, and she hadn't eaten it in years.

"I can tell you don't, but you haven't tried mine yet." He set a plate in front of her. Steak, mashed potatoes, and a vegetable mix. He brought over a loaf of quick bread and cut a slice for both of them.

Feeling like a jerk for teasing him before, she said, "Brent, this is really nice."

He poured wine in their glasses and sat down, his eyes gleaming. "Try the steak."

She cut a piece and planned to lie if it wasn't the best steak she ever had. But the flavor hit her and her eyes went wide.

His sexy grin flashed. "Told you."

She knew she looked sheepish, but didn't care. She savored several bites before trying the potatoes.

Brent sliced the bread and buttered a piece for both of them. "Try this, then you'll know you owe me."

The steak blew her away, but the bread did her in. "There's no way you made this."

"Why not?" He buttered another piece for himself. This guy could do anything and look sexy. While they ate, she tried to keep from staring at his mouth, his hands. Her only consolation was he looked at her as much as she eyed him. Course, he'd been doing that since they met.

He finished off his dinner and asked, "So what do you really think of working here?"

She paused with her hand halfway to her mouth with another bite of bread. "Oh, so you're doing this to get some info out of me?"

"Just being neighborly is all." He didn't let his smile fade. Oh, she'd been an idiot. She drank the last of her wine before she answered.

"I'm sore all over," she said. Instantly she wanted to slap herself for being so honest, and saying something like that to him.

"I can help with that."

*I bet you could.* She looked down at his hands, so nice and big. And strong. He'd caught her looking again. He stood, making her nervous, and moved behind her chair, even while she shook her head in horror. She could count the few times they'd touched so far, and each time sent her body in agony. Or paradise. She couldn't tell.

"Brent . . ."

"Relax." His hands slid around her arms, holding her the way he had the day he taught her to ride a horse. She held her breath, held herself still.

She bit into her lip and closed her eyes. Don't moan! His hands moved up to her shoulders, applying light pressure, kneading. He worked his way in from her shoulders to the base of her neck and gradually increased the pressure. Unable to fight, she leaned her head forward.

"You're . . . good at this."

His thumbs ran up her neck and down to her back again. She'd been right about his big hands. They could do magic. It'd been so long since someone had touched her like this, taking care of her.

His warm hands moved under the collar of her shirt. Heat spiked up in her, taking away her willpower. She gave in, surrendered, and whimpered.

Oh, no!

"That good, huh?"

His voice flowed over her like honey. She could cry. Her mind wouldn't work except to think, *don't ever stop.*

He rubbed and kneaded until her head fell back. His hands were affecting other parts of her body, places where he wasn't actually touching. What if he could tell?

As if he sensed he was taking her too far, he squeezed her neck once more, then she heard him sit in the chair next to her.

She was sure she wouldn't be able to look at him, but when she opened her eyes, he looked soft, tender. Now, more than ever, she wanted his hands on the rest of her.

If her voice worked, she'd thank him, but she couldn't do anything but stare at him.

"Do you think you can manage to walk home?" He stood and traced the outside of his hand down her face. "Or I could carry you."

Carry her? No way. Stumbling, she got to her feet and shook her head. "I can't let you do that."

He followed her to the door, where she spun around. Her mind had cleared. "The mess. I should help you clean."

He just shook his head. "I'll walk you home. You look tired."

What did he mean by that? She wouldn't let him in, no matter how good his hands had felt. Her neck and shoulders still felt warm and loose.

"Dinner was great," she conceded.

Stopping by the front closet, they wrapped up before he opened the door. "So no more teasing about the banjo or crock pot?"

She burst out laughing. "Oh, no. I've got a buzz."

He shut the door behind her. "From one glass of wine?"

One glass? He was right, so why did she feel so light and carefree? Once they were down the steps, he walked next to her and put his arm across her shoulders. She shivered from the cold and leaned into him.

"I'm sorry I teased you before," she said. He smelled so good, she wanted to turn her face into his chest and take a deep breath. They were quiet on the walk. She wasn't sure why he was quiet, but she felt so relaxed, she couldn't think.

He walked her up to the door and opened it for her. She searched for a way to tell him she wasn't ready to invite him in. While she thought about it, his other arm slid around her.

Her body willingly relaxed in his arms, but her mind screamed. What was she doing?

He kissed the top of her head and stepped back. She met his gaze and then wished she hadn't.

"You're something else, Missy."

She managed a confused expression.

"You can trust me. Promise." He turned and went down the steps, waving on his way back on the road.

*You can trust me.* How could he promise that? And how did he even know she was afraid to?

\* \* \* \*

The next morning, Brent awoke and moved, turning onto his side in bed before jolting up. His side felt great! He was back in the game. He didn't hear rain coming down outside, so maybe it'd be clear today.

Even though he'd been back on his feet the last few days, Dale and Ivan hadn't allowed him to help with anything. He didn't pull rank and tell them it was his ranch, because he knew they meant well. Doctor's orders and all. But, darn it, it'd been hard to see Missy when he couldn't work.

He'd known if he allowed himself to get involved with her, she'd break his heart. The thought still tormented him, but now he knew he wouldn't fight it. If she was going to be here, there was only one way to do it. If he didn't get her in his bed soon, he'd never get his work done.

With that decision made, he threw back the covers, his mission clear in his head.

He'd been using warm showers to help his injured muscles relax. After another one, he didn't bother with coffee or breakfast in his haste to get outside. In the pasture, he spotted Missy and Dale in the soup-like fog. He'd almost reached them before they heard him coming.

"Hi." Missy watched the way he walked, just like a worried mother would. "How's the side?"

"Great. I don't think I can take another day of resting." He waved as Dale started off. Her coat, he saw now, wasn't red but burgundy. He wouldn't normally notice a thing like that, but the color went perfectly with her skin tone. "I appreciate the way you've helped out around here."

"That's why I'm here." She nudged his arm. "Remember?"

"You've certainly proved yourself."

She gave him her beautiful smile, making him notice even more her full, deep red lips. Her hair hung loose and wild, framing her face in a way that made her cheekbones gracefully noticeable.

"Really? You think I'm ranch material now?"

"You can pull your own, that's all I'm saying." He tried to hide his grin, but couldn't help it anymore. And he didn't care. She'd done more than prove herself.

She glanced up and caught him watching her. Her smile wavered before she looked away. Skittish as a colt, but he'd win her over.

Jeffery trotted up and bumped Brent with his nose while making horse murmurs and pawing at the ground. "Itching for a ride? Me, too."

Missy raised her eyebrows at him.

"I'm fine." He wanted to go on a ride with her and enjoy the morning as the sun burned off the fog. Though the ground was soggy, Brent thought they could stick to the gravel road. "Besides, I'll have to go slow so you can keep up."

He turned and started for the stables to get their tack. He'd seen her eyes narrow, and he didn't need another injury now, right when he was up to full speed. Jeffery came behind him, and he thought he heard Missy huff a sigh and follow suit. Whistling, he got both saddles and readied their horses.

"Here, you lead her out." He handed her Speckle's reins. "Did you ride much this week? I hardly saw you around here."

"Some." She swung up into her saddle, as though she'd been riding for years, not days.

He mounted and they started off together. "Missy, I'm sorry for the cold way I acted when you came here."

Her eyes went wide and her brows rose.

"Never heard an apology before?" he teased. They rode side by side out toward the main road, and he didn't press her to say anything. He could see her relax as they rode and he enjoyed just having her beside him, doing something they both loved. "Look at you, a natural already."

"A natural?" She patted her horse. "I guess I do enjoy riding. Sure wasn't easy that first day!" He joined in her laughing, mostly because he loved the light and carefree sound she made. Enchanted, he couldn't help but be encouraged.

"So, have you worked things out with your boyfriend?" Now that thought had popped into his mind and out his mouth. During the last week, he'd spent far too much time wondering if she still talked to the man she'd left, if she thought about him, and if she planned to go back to him.

Her quick cutting look proved he'd been a real jerk to ask. "What boyfriend would that be?"

"Your boss. Sounded like you had a fight before you came out here."

"It was over before I came out here, and I don't plan on ever speaking with him again." She nudged the horse ahead, leaving him to watch her hair shimmer in the weak sunlight that made it through the morning fog.

The light vanished and he looked up. The fog was dissipating, but a front of dark clouds followed behind. He usually saw a storm coming, so he wasn't happy that she'd distracted him.

"It's about to break loose," he told her just as a brisk wind flipped her hair around. She followed his lead and turned her horse to head back.

\* \* \* \*

In the stables, Brent moved the brush across Jeffrey's back with long, sweeping stokes. "I shouldn't have asked."

"It's fine." She shrugged without looking at him. "But if we're going to be friends, we can't do that."

"Do what?" And why did they need to stick to friendship? How could they deny what they felt?

"Ask questions."

"Why not?" His hand paused as he looked at her. "Friends do that." Her face was guarded, setting him on edge.

"Ok, fine, but my past is off limits. I'm sure by now you understand it's too hard for me to talk about." When she pulled in a deep breath, he noticed her hands tremble on the horse.

Speckle made a loving noise as if she felt Missy's fear, and Brent felt awful for causing it.

"I'm sorry. Listen, I'll try to keep to that, and if I mess up, just tell me."

She smiled. "Thanks."

He stepped closer so that when she turned, she was inches from him. They stood close enough for him to smell her lavender shampoo.

Confusion washed across her face before understanding.

"You change gears awful fast." Her try at lightness failed and her voice came out heavy, husky.

"Think so?" His voice grew as quiet as it could without becoming a whisper. "If you don't want to kiss me, you'd better run. Now."

# Chapter Five

She had to be imaging the care in his eyes. This hadn't been her goal. So when had these feelings snuck in?

He hovered, obviously waiting for her to either make a move or run.

He wasn't her boss this time, but close enough. Wasn't she here to prove she could make it on a ranch? She wanted to turn away, but leaned closer instead.

Weren't his eyes magnificent? She thought of a clear winter sky, so freshly light blue. His eyes searched hers, searched her face as if to memorize, and settled on her mouth. Oh, no, her mouth was open, her lip trembling.

*Get a grip, Missy! Get a grip and run!* No, no, no, why was she leaning forward? Her heart hammered as his head tilted, leaned, and then it happened. Their lips met.

Something sharp and sweet washed through her, starting at her mouth and running down to her feet. His lips moved against hers and she nearly jumped. She would have, if she could move.

She was timid and he seemed to feel it. Though their tongues touched lightly, he kept space between their bodies. He rested one hand on her arm and nothing more.

That made her want more of him.

Brent tasted like the outdoors, sweet like autumn sunshine and country air. The smell of his leather coat and his aftershave racked through her. She'd never smelled anything like it.

Or felt anything like his lips on hers, so tender and asking. She reached up and found his shoulders with her hands and leaned closer. She'd lost control. His arms came around her, encircling the dip of her waist. She ached for him, wanted his hands to tease lightly all over her bare skin, but she knew better. She could lose everything again. What was she doing?

Sanity raised its troubling head and she pushed out of Brent's hold. She shouldn't have kissed him.

She'd vowed to never again get involved with someone she worked with. Not after the struggle to get past the humiliation and the rumors. She turned and ran clear to her house.

\* \* \* \*

"Missy!"

She didn't hear. She was gone.

His body felt on fire. For a minute, he'd been lost in the most moving experience of his life. His lips felt cold now that hers weren't there.

Was he loosing it, or had she leaned toward him first? The woman had no idea of what she wanted. Her reaction sent a chill through him, though he couldn't tell if she'd been shocked or disgusted. Both were disheartening.

He breathed deeply and debated for a minute, and then started walking. Maybe it wouldn't be as simple as getting her into bed. He had tried to tell himself that would fix these feelings for both of them so they could get on with their work.

But she was afraid of something, and he felt a lot more than plain old lust.

If only he knew what to do about it. For the moment, he needed to make sure she was okay. He knocked five times before she opened the door. The words he wanted to say just didn't work. Not when he saw the pain in her big brown eyes.

She'd removed her red coat, revealing the white long sleeve shirt she wore underneath. It stretched across her breasts, making him wish they were here to continue what they'd started, not discuss why they wouldn't be.

Something big stood in the way of her trusting him. He could see it in his expression. Her pale face made her eyes larger, darker. He wanted to hold her and kiss her again to make it all right, but not after what just happened.

"Missy, don't you trust me?"

Taking several steps back, she nodded. At the very least, she said she did. Maybe she'd been upset with herself for breaking a personal rule. Could it be that simple?

"Then did I read you wrong?" he asked, stepping inside and shutting the door.

"No." Her hunched shoulders kept him close to the door, watching her as she took a deep breath. When she motioned to the couch, he came in and sat, leaving space between them.

Suddenly he noticed the pile of folded blankets next to the couch. "You're sleeping out here?"

Shrugging, she tried to say something, but just ran her fingers through her hair. He didn't understand for a minute, but it didn't take long.

From where he sat, he could see down the hallway, to the bedroom door. It was shut. He doubted she'd gone into Ben's old room.

Brent felt so lousy about himself he didn't know what to say.

She cleared her throat. "I'm sorry."

Even if she'd kissed him first, which he doubted now, it wasn't her fault. "You don't have to be sorry for it."

She looked up to his face again. He saw regret in her eyes and braced for the words. "I have to be, and I can't do that again."

"You didn't like it?" His question went over the line, but he had to know. He wasn't sure how he'd walk away from someone so mysterious, so beautiful.

"I did like kissing you, Brent." The way she spoke slowly had him bracing for the 'but'. "I'm just not ready for a relationship."

"I wasn't either. There's no way to prepare for that." She'd about knocked him over, sent him into moans.

"I don't think I'll ever be ready for that." She stood back up as she spoke, and he jumped to his feet after her.

"If you're not attracted to me, tell me, but please don't turn away if it's something else."

She folded her arms. "I don't have to explain this to you, or anybody. I told you my problems are just that, remember? My problems." Anger simmered under her quick words. She took three long strides to the door and grabbed the handle.

She was tall, but he was taller and took two steps to catch her. He planted a hand on top of hers. "That's not how it works with people who care about you."

"What?"

"Yeah, I care about you." Without warning, he planted his mouth on hers again. She made a noise that started like an *hmm* and ended with an *ahh*! She leaned into him, going soft, her hands relaxing on his shoulders, but it ended quickly. With a shove, she separated them.

Eyes dancing with fury and heat, she declared, "I don't have to kiss you, and I don't have to explain!"

Taking her gently by the chin, he held her so she looked straight into his eyes. "Of course you don't have to kiss me. But since you did back there, you should tell me why you don't want to do it again."

"No!" She shook, trying not to cry. "I can't."

"Why, Missy? What happened that made you this way? Because your boss lied about you, or because he did something else?"

She stared at him with icy eyes.

"He hurt you?" Sure, he was blunt. He'd always been that way. But he regretted this instance of it because the emotion slid off her face. He'd lost her.

Instead of responding, she passed him and walked down the hall. Man, he needed to learn how to talk to people. He went to the bathroom door where she'd locked herself in.

"I'm sorry, Missy."

She answered with silence.

"I'm too curious for my own good." He resigned himself to talking to the door. "I've grown to care about you. It happened when we met, but I didn't want to like you. I can't fight it now. So I'm sorry about whatever happened."

Wow, his longest speech ever. He heard quiet crying and nothing else.

"I hold on too tight, I know." Confession time now, he guessed. "I don't want to push you away. I don't want to lose you, too." She didn't answer and he was out of words.

Now what? He could hear her crying and couldn't do a damn thing about it.

Sure, he could sit and wait. Or he could remember his place, or more specifically that this was her place now, her home.

"Okay, I'm leaving, but I won't give up on you." His legs felt stiff on his way out, like he had to push through river water to get outside.

He gulped down a cool breath of sweet Oregon air. This complicated the hell out of things, but there was no turning back.

\* \* \* \*

"Has there been a flash flood warning?" Dale asked as he met Brent at the stable entrance in the early morning.

"Not officially, but I feel something coming. Let's get the rest of the horses in." He'd brought in two already, but he needed help to calm down the horses remaining in the pasture.

They were excited about something, and it just might be the heavy rain they'd had for days now.

The horses couldn't seem to make up their minds once they were inside for the day. They settled down, then panicked again.

"It's just rain," he muttered to himself before the truth hit him. His mood, not the weather, was spooking them.

He trudged back to the pasture. How was he supposed to act normal? He wanted to help Missy

through this, whatever it was. Plus, they couldn't work together with things the way they were.
With the horses in their stalls, he felt better.

"Brent?" That one quiet word behind him made him jump. He turned around to find Missy bundled in a thick brown jacket, her arms crossed and pulled close.

He stood, staring, a full minute at her lips, red from the cold, and her weepy eyes. They were wide, driving him crazy, and reminding him he should answer.

"Missy." He stepped closer, gauging her reaction, but she didn't move.

"I'm sorry I shut you out like that." She dropped her gaze.

"No, I am. I said the wrong thing." This felt like a second chance to talk things out, but he knew to step lightly. He wondered if he could at least offer a hand of support on her shoulder.

She was trying not to cry and needed something. So he took the last step, but stopped in front of her, not touching, just waiting. "Well, if we're both sorry, let's just move on. If you want to, that is."

When she nodded, he moved his arm across her back and drew her closer. That sweet lavender smell reached him right before she relaxed into him. Her head leaned and rested on his shoulder.

"Can we be friends again?" she asked. Feeling her in his arms stirred protective feelings. She felt like a fragile fawn, too wobbly to stand on its new legs. Her lavender and spice scent stirred other things, but he ignored them.

"Friends, Missy." *And anything else you want from me.* He hoped she sensed that thought because speaking it wouldn't be right.

He couldn't fight for a woman who asked him for his friendship. She clearly needed that, someone to depend on. He could be a good friend, it had always been the *more* that caused problems.

\* \* \* \*

After she looked out her window the next morning and saw Brent working with horses, Missy stayed indoors for the day. Somehow she had to keep busy and not think about their kisses.

The cabin had no TV, so she tried to finish the cleaning. She'd added some touches of her own here and there, though she'd been hesitant to replace Ben's things with her own.

Coming here turned her life around. She'd spent three years thinking about the firm, her accounts, building her reputation. She'd fought and won battles.

Now she questioned what she'd been fighting for. Whatever she sought before, wasn't there.

She stood by the window that faced down the road, toward Brent's house. She couldn't see it.

After glancing around the empty cabin, she went outside for a walk. It was eleven, and she saw Dale and Ivan working on the fence Brent was adding to section off the pasture.

She needed to talk to them, without Brent around. What better way to befriend two men than with food? She headed inside to fix something. Twenty minutes later, she brought them hot drinks and sandwiches and hung around to hear their rodeo stories.

Halfway through Dale's recounting of the time he broke four ribs, she heard Brent's giant truck hauling down the gravel road. She knew she wouldn't get out of there in time without being rude, and that would undo her efforts with the men.

He pulled the truck up by his house and headed their way. Why should she avoid him? She'd never felt so safe with anyone else.

She watched him walk, watched his long jean-clad legs. He was dependable about those jeans. Every day she got to drool over him in them.

Teasing aside, he was patient. He gave great massages. Cooked her a wonderful dinner. And every time, he walked her home without making a move. Until that kiss.

She met his gaze, wondering if he could tell what she was thinking about.

"So this is what I miss when I head into town for a day?"

"You should take off more often." Ivan grinned over his sandwich.

Brent gave her a look.

"I wasn't sure what to do with myself. You weren't here handing out chores." She tried for the light tone that their teasing had carried before, but when her gaze met his, she could tell he wouldn't see her as an annoying city girl ever again.

Dale and Ivan both seemed to miss his lack of response and jumped knee-deep into conversation about getting the fence finished before the rain came back.

"Thanks for lunch, Missy," Dale said as the two men headed back to work.

"Seems they like you."

"I try." She picked up the tray and mugs.

"Listen, you don't need me telling you what to do. If you want to join them, go ahead. Or go for a ride. Feed the horses."

"Are you tired of bossing me around?" She gave him a grin, but he saw through it.

"You don't need bossing around." He tipped his hat and turned to leave.

Just like that? She watched him go, sinking inside. Why wasn't she happy that he listened to her? First time she'd ever gotten a man to do what she wanted, and it didn't want to make her dance around. Darn him!

She took the dishes back to the house before she headed down to the stables. If she'd learned anything, it was how to muck out a stall, so she took on the dirty job with a vengeance.

Did he think she wanted space? Yeah, she'd asked to be friends, and that meant she wanted to spend time around him.

She needed him.

Where did that come from? She didn't need anyone.

\* \* \* \*

Look at that. Her hair flying and dancing with the horse's gait, Missy rode Speckle with an ease that usually came with years of riding. The smile, too, went with a deep love of horses and joy of riding.

Maybe she hadn't grown up in the lifestyle, but it suited her. And he'd never seen anyone look as good as she did on a horse. Relaxed, in rhythm, and graceful.

She'd been all over the property lately, and he hoped it was to look for him. He stepped away from the corner of the stables and raised a hand.

She turned Speckle and trotted up, a cautious smile on her face.

"Brent." She wore that burgundy sweater that made him want to touch her. While its color put a rose tone to her skin, it clung to her in all the right places.

"Howdy, stranger." Brent almost grinned when he thought of what his friends would say about him using reverse psychology.

Missy didn't want him to push her or ask about her past, so he wouldn't. His quiet, steady way would win her over. Not that his emotion about her felt quiet in any way. Working with her day after day made them louder and louder, harder to control.

"Taking her in?" he asked, shoving his hands into his coat pockets to keep them warm.

"Yeah. What are you up to?" She swung down and led Speckle into the stable yard.

"Just hanging around," he said, keeping it vague, and managed to keep the grin off his face as he walked in with her. She didn't need to know how glad he was to see her again.

She looked amazing as she fed and brushed the horse. So natural and caring. When she led Speckle back into her stall, the rain suddenly came down hard enough to make a thundering sound through the stable roof.

"I was thinking about my brother," she said as she moved on to pet a different horse. He busied himself by bringing hay over.

"I've done some of that lately." He kept his tone light, but those weren't words with a light meaning.

"Do you miss him?" she asked, then answered herself. "Of course you do. I'm sorry if it's hard having me here, instead of him."

He stopped to look at her. "Listen, the circumstances aren't great, but I'm glad you're here."

"You are?" She turned this time, and her eyes had that same lost look he'd seen the first time they spoke. "I wish I'd gotten my priorities straight and come for a visit sooner. He invited me. I guess you don't know that since he didn't even tell you about me." She turned back to her work.

"Missy, he didn't tell me about the rest of his life. That's how men are. He didn't know much about me before we became friends. Even when Amanda left, he didn't ask me to explain."

"Amanda?"

Shoot, he'd just blown the mood, and now he had to explain. "She's the reason I have that house. She was a part of this when it started, but she took off after two months. I guess that's why I thought you'd see life on a ranch and head back to the city."

"One woman, all women, huh? I've made the same mistake about men." She flicked a look over at him, and he decided to take that as apology for her turning him out the other day. He'd heard enough to know her old boss had taken advantage of her.

"So are you heading anywhere for Thanksgiving?"

She looked surprised at the change in subject, but didn't call him on it.

"I don't do much for any holiday. Maybe watch football."

Was he supposed to laugh at that? He'd never heard of a woman who didn't celebrate the holidays. "I wasn't sure if you have family in the area."

"I don't have family anywhere, not anymore." She moved on to a new horse and began to brush, as if this wasn't a heavy conversation. But it wasn't the weather and it did matter.

"I guess I forgot to tell you." He started talking while he thought it through. "If you're here on the ranch, you have to celebrate with us."

"That's a ranch rule?"

"Yup. Dale and Ivan and me, we all thought maybe we could get the little woman to cook for us."

She whipped around and threw hay at him. "So that's what this is about?"

"Well, we'll all pitch in. Isn't that the true spirit of Thanksgiving? We can cook at my house. Watch the game. Drink some beer. It'll be fun."

A smile brightened her face, warming her eyes as well. It was the first real smile he'd seen on her since before they'd kissed and that was something he shouldn't be thinking about. If he wanted her to feel comfortable about joining them, he needed to be a friend.

"Well . . ." she said, biting her lip. Keeping his gaze off her mouth, he decided he could be a gentleman for a day. Not think about her lips, or brown eyes, or that petite body.

"Make that a yes, and I'll buy the turkey and everything to go with it."

"I actually can cook a turkey," she said. He lifted his brows in disbelief. "I can. I'm better at big dinners than preparing an everyday meal. Just wait and see."

He had her. Or so he thought. Maybe she had him.

## Chapter Six

At the rumble outside at eight in the morning, Missy went to the window and found Brent turning off his truck and stepping out. Why did the man have to be so breathtaking? So cool and hot at the same time?

She opened the door. "That's an awful big alarm clock."

"Weren't you up?"

"Yeah, I was." Barely. She'd just finished breakfast. "What's up?"

There had to be a reason he had his truck here. He nudged his hat back and walked up the steps. "If it's okay with you, I'll haul off some of this junk."

"Oh." They both knew the junk meant Ben's things, but she could see in his face that he needed to keep it light if he was going to do this. "That'd be fine. I put everything I don't need in his bedroom."

"Mind if I look through all of it?"

She wanted to wrap her arms around him as she sensed his pain. "Of course. You don't have to ask me that."

They'd talked about hauling all the papers off to the dump, but she hadn't rushed him on it. She carried out the smaller boxes while he took the heavier ones. Brent didn't stop to look at anything until they came across a box full of photos in the bedroom.

She paused in the doorway when she saw him, sitting on the floor to look through the pictures. Leaving quietly, she waited in the living room. Twenty minutes passed before he carried the box out. She didn't plan to say anything about it, but he stopped beside her.

"You might want to keep that one." He handed her a picture.

It showed her standing beside Ben, both with uncertain smiles on their faces.

"Thanks . . . this is when we met. We didn't know what to think of each other."

Her emotions seemed in check till she heard her shaky breathing. His arms came around her in that instant and she didn't debate this time before falling into his arms.

His breath came out shaky, too. She cried for a brother she hardly knew . . . while he mourned a friend. Thank heaven he never pointed that out, not since the first day.

Those thoughts dropped from her mind when she smelled his freshness from a shower, the soapy smell of his skin. His well-toned body felt strong against her. Minutes slipped by and she didn't care, not with her eyes closed and their hearts beating against each other.

"Well . . . I should get going. I'll be back, though."

* * * *

Three hours later, Brent backed his truck up to Missy's steps so they could unload the bed he'd bought. Missy still hadn't gone into Ben's room, so he wanted to get her a new bed. Maybe that would help. Finding it hadn't taken three hours, but he'd needed some time to think about what he'd found in Ben's things.

He turned off the truck's engine and looked down at the papers in the seat beside him.

A will. His messy, unorganized friend had started a will. Since it was hand written, and not notarized, it might not stand up legally, but it had been Ben's wishes just the same. Now what would he do with it?

If Missy read it, she might leave.

The front door of the house creaked and he stuffed the papers in his glove compartment. Hitching an arm out the window, he watched her walk down the steps.

"You didn't have to do this." She pulled on her red coat. He stepped out and met her at the back of the truck.

"I wanted to." The wind caught her hair and whipped it in her face. He watched the silky strands feather on the breeze, then pushed aside his fascination with her hair to answer, "It's overdue. I shouldn't have left you with all of Ben's things."

He knew Ben had been her brother, but since she hadn't known him all that well, this was his responsibility.

"I'll pay you back."

"No need." He stared at her too long.

She shifted her weight, signaling her discomfort, so he lowered the tailgate and they carried it inside together.

They worked well together, whether caring for the horses or moving furniture.

Just imagine what they could do . . . together . . . in the bedroom.

He stood back, looking at the bed, all ready with the mattresses on it. They were alone in her bedroom, and his mind wouldn't behave.

"Brent?" Missy asked, her voice soft and shy. Biting his tongue, he hoped she hadn't caught the look in his face as he imagined them naked together on the bed.

Turning, she looked unsure of herself with a little smile tugging at her lips. He lost the power to think as he looked at her, those lips and big brown eyes full of questions, so he raised his eyebrows and made a noise.

"I haven't been horseback riding on the beach yet."

"No?" he asked, wanting to stare at her all day, but he noticed her smile fade. Oh, yeah, time to answer the question. "Sure, we can go. Is now okay?"

She flashed him a relieved smile. "We could pack a lunch," she suggested.

Hiding his own smile, he said, "I'll fix it."

When he teased her, her unease seemed to melt and she nudged his arm. They left her bedroom, grabbed their coats, and headed for his house.

This being friendly worked out pretty well, except for when his imagination put together different scenarios of how he could get her clothes off.

She wandered around while he fixed sandwiches. When he didn't hear her, he stepped to the hallway and saw her looking at the fireplace - his favorite place in the house.

He liked to sit there with a beer, watch the flames, or read a magazine. Though, with Missy with him, he'd have different things to do.

Almost laughing at himself, he turned to finish making their lunch. They needed to hurry so they could have some daylight to enjoy the beach.

"Ready?" he called as he retrieved their coats from the closest. He grabbed a ski cap he kept on the closet shelf and pulled it on her head when she came over.

"You might want that. The wind can give you an ache in your ears and jaw."

"Thanks," she said, fingering the wooly material. It came down to her brows, framing her face. She didn't seem to know how beautiful she looked. Or she didn't until she saw the look on his face. He could tell she noticed when her cheeks turned pink.

He gave her hair a gentle tug and opened the door. For one second, he wondered if she would stay around or run off. But he ignored the thought, choosing to enjoy the day. They headed to the pasture where the horses were grazing.

"I can tell why we separate the stallion from the mares, but why do you keep the geldings apart?" she asked as they reached the fence.

"They can still try to pull rank. The stallion will fight the geldings, too." He paused to open the gate. Several horses came toward them, including Jeffery and Speckle. "I like to play it safe since we take on boarder horses. The last thing our reputation needs is a wounded boarder."

They led their horses to the stables to saddle them. When her gaze met his, he felt an immediate physical reaction, right where she could see it if she looked down. She sure could turn him on, but he didn't let her know. No, he wanted her to trust him.

Since it'd reached late afternoon already, he picked up the pace along the trail. "How does it feel?" he asked.

"Fine. Speckle shows me what to do."

That was what he wanted to hear. "We keep a slow pace when we take tourists out, but I don't want to be too late today. Wouldn't do for Speckle to stumble in the dark and pitch you on your heard."

Mist came in from the river. It added more moisture to the air, making it feel thick and heavy. A soft silence enveloped the forest except for the noise they made.

As they neared the top of the hill, he slowed so they could see the ocean. Today the mist blocked most of their view.

Brent glanced at Missy as they guided the horses down the beach trail. She sat comfortably in the saddle, although focused on the trail.

"Nice work," he told her. "You've got it."

Scotch Broom bushes lined the path until the bottom of the trail before it opened and they were on the beach. Missy pulled in a breath at the view. Sand stretched out all around them and waves pounded the beach ahead.

Pulling up beside him, she said, "It's loud."

He liked the wonder in her eyes, and how red her lips were from the cold air. It took him a minute to see she had turned her gaze to him.

"I've been biting my tongue and not telling you how beautiful you are," he said with reverence. There wasn't any change in her expression, but she didn't look away, either. "Caught you by surprise?" he asked.

*A Cowboy For Christmas*

She laughed. "You do that a lot." Her breathless voice stirred his passion. Should he tell her what she did to him?

No, he'd learned his lesson when he rushed her before, so he'd take it slow. "Want to ride down the beach a ways?"

Excitement lit up her eyes. She nudged Speckle and they set off, nice and slow to enjoy the ocean. He'd been around the cold ocean, the sea gulls, the foghorns all his life, but he could tell it was new for her. She watched the birds as they swooped and darted over the endless banter of water and sand.

"Here comes a big one," he said.

"How do you know?"

"It'll be the seventh. Everything's got a pattern." He paused alongside her horse. The next wave rose up higher, crashed, and came racing up the sand.

"It's going to get us!" She backed her horse up. Speckle flicked an ear, and looked at him as if to say, *She's a newbie.* The wave did reach them, but the horses weren't afraid of the ocean.

A bank of fog hung in the air above them, leaving stillness underneath. Even while the ocean fought the land, the air stood still.

"Where did the wind go?" she asked him.

"It does this once in a while, fall or springtime." He'd walked it all his life, but today was new for him. Today was with her.

She glanced at him and smiled.

"Hungry?" he asked. At her nod, he led the way back toward the brush near the hill. Staying by the horses, they sat on the sand with the sandwiches.

"Thanks for today," she said before taking a bite. After chewing for a minute she added, "For the furniture, and all this."

"My pleasure." He meant that, too, in a big way. Watching her ride, watching her watch him back. It was all his pleasure.

A desperate need filled him. He wanted to kiss her, but he'd been unable to gauge if that's what she wanted.

While they ate, she turned her gaze toward the waves and sky. Hardly a soul had ventured out today. That could have something to do with the fading daylight and falling temperatures.

The fog made it seem later, darker, and he knew they should head back. He didn't want her riding up the hill for the first time in the dark.

She turned to him. "It's almost dark."

"Yeah, time to go," he agreed and stood, offering his hand. Hers felt cold, another reason to leave.

When she stood, her body nearly brushed his. At first, she looked at his chin. He knew she could sense the mood, sense how he watched her.

She raised her gaze to meet his. After a searching, thoughtful look, she rose on her toes and softly kissed his cheek.

The woman was killing him.

She mounted her horse and waited for him. Yeah, he'd follow her anywhere. But would she let him? Did she want to stay with him? He couldn't even tell if this was the start of something or just a nice day for her.

He let her lead the way back up the hill and through the forest. They didn't speak. How could they?

*A Cowboy For Christmas*

He felt something like respect for the time, for that kiss, and for the feelings that must be boiling inside her. He wanted to take it slow, for her.

After they brushed the horses, he walked her home. Her mind seemed to be turning something over, and he hoped it was him. She glanced at him several times, but didn't say much.

At her door, he leaned in and brushed his lips across hers. If lightening could touch lightly, it did.

The look in her eyes asked for more. Instead, he touched his hat and headed back to the stables. The horses needed their blankets since the temperature was already flirting with freezing.

He smiled on his way there because he'd tricked her into taking an evening off. Tomorrow was Thanksgiving, and he planned to take full advantage of having her in his house all day. She'd need her rest tonight.

\* \* \* \*

Missy rolled over onto her back, rubbed her hair out of her face, and stretched. The alarm clock clicked on and Alan Jackson's smooth, sweet voice filled the room. "Good morning to you, too. And happy Thanksgiving!"

She sat up on the edge of the bed - the new one Brent had brought back for her - to listen to the rest of the song before turning if off. She'd changed everything about herself when she moved to Las Vegas, everything except her love of country music, which she'd hidden.

She hadn't sung in the shower in a while. She did today while lathering on coconut body wash and extra conditioner in her hair. When she dressed, she pulled on an olive green sweater that Brent hadn't seen yet.

Since coming to the ranch, she hadn't been applying as much makeup, but today she went all the way. She was about to leave the bathroom when she decided to pull her hair up.

Daylight met her outside, soft and innocent as she walked through the thin mist. Promising. A fuzzy yellow spot indicated where the sun was above the tree line. Maybe the mist would burn off to a nice day.

Had Brent meant what she'd read in his eyes? Did she trust him? She couldn't imagine him using her feelings against her, but she couldn't let go of that fear, either.

She wore new leather boots and Levis. It didn't compare to how she'd dressed for her old job, but this fit in with Brent and his friends.

She knocked and wrapped her arms around herself while she waited. The door swung open and Brent's cologne kicked her in the stomach with a sensation she . . . might like.

"What are you knocking for?" he asked, his blue eyes full of teasing and desire at the same time. The look put her mind into sex mode before she could stop it.

"Right. I still need to catch you in the shower." *Or climbing out, skin damp with a towel around his waist.* His pupils widened. Then, leaning close, he kissed her cheek. Rather, he kissed her right next to her mouth. And that was worse than kissing her lips, because now she itched all over to touch him.

"You look nice." He held the door open.

"Nice?" she teased with a small smile.

*A Cowboy For Christmas*

"You always look nice. I was being polite, but I could have said you look good enough to eat. Or lick, whichever."

She blushed at that one, and could tell that's what he wanted. Their eyes met, and his were full of playfulness. He looked pretty yummy himself, but she lost her nerve and didn't say so. His snug jeans and fitted black T-shirt were driving her crazy, but she didn't plan on telling him what she wanted to do.

When she followed him into the kitchen, she saw brown grocery bags all over his counter. "I got everything on your list and then some," he said.

"I can see that." She had to look away from the sexy grin he flashed her. He started to pull things from the freezer and refrigerator. Looking inside the bags, she saw they contained all the nonperishable items she could ever want for a fest.

She looked at him again and her heart beat wildly in her chest. That black shirt of his did something to her. So did the view as she stood behind him, checking out his butt in the jeans.

"Here you go." She brought over chopped celery and onion. When she turned her back to chop mushrooms, she felt his lips touch her neck. Moist and warm, his kiss sent pleasure rocketing through her body.

"I'm trying to work here," she murmured

"And I'm trying to seduce you." His soft voice tickled her ear, so she laughed instead of responding. When he stepped back, she was glad she had a minute to get her bearings. He wanted to seduce her?

Did that mean, seduce her and have a relationship?

~ 91 ~

They both heard loud, feminine laughter from outside, and Brent smiled. "That'd be Alice, Dale's girlfriend."

When she took a shaky breath, he turned and went to the door.

She followed hesitantly, realizing something was happening. Maybe it had been happening for a while, but she wasn't fighting as fiercely as she usually did. Being on the ranch at first had been one thing, but to feel welcome was another thing.

"Dale, Alice." Brent greeted them as he opened the door. "Alice, this is Missy."

"Well, well. Now I see why Brent let that horse kick him."

Missy shot Brent a confused look. Did she have something to do with that? Dale and Alice both hooted while she narrowed her eyes at Brent.

"We saw Ivan coming down the road," Dale said, most likely to change the subject for Brent's sake, then went to the door to open it.

\* \* \* \*

Brent left the living room where everyone chatted but returned a moment later with his violin. "I promised the lady a song or two, for taking care of me while my side healed up."

He held her gaze while he warmed up. Next he eased into a soulful piece, with beautiful soaring passages. His hands moved expertly, showing years of practice, and his love of the instrument came through in his playing.

With his intense gaze on her, she couldn't look away from him. Even while she knew everyone looked between her and him.

She no longer knew what to expect from his man - except that she had a lot more to learn.

## Chapter Seven

Music had been a hobby, one he'd always enjoyed, but tonight his music became a love song for Missy. He put his feelings for her into his music, hoping she understood his longing, his need to touch her, his need to take her breath away.

The others clapped along with her when he finished the last song, but he looked into her wondrous brown eyes only, gauging her response.

*Romance, anyone?*

To everyone he said, "Smells like dinner's done." He didn't want to make a big show of it, and he'd seen what he wanted from Missy. She'd listened with more than her ears, leaning forward, her face enraptured.

After he carried the turkey to the table, he carved while everyone filled their plates.

"Did you cook for the rest of the year?" Alice asked Brent with a laugh, "You don't think we eat this much, do you?"

He shrugged and glanced at Missy. She returned his smile with a secretive one, a shared look. With her hair pulled up, she looked different. Sophisticated, but not aloof like when he'd first met her. It helped that she wore a soft green sweater and not a silk suit.

Funny thing was, he itched to pull her hair free and watch it tumble down around her shoulders -- after kissing her neck like crazy. He hadn't thought of that. Maybe he liked it up . . . for a while.

"Gonna daydream all day, or are you hungry?" Dale intruded into his fantasy. One look at Dale grinning at him told Brent his thoughts were pretty apparent.

"Don't wait for me, dig in," he joked right back. He didn't care if everyone could tell what was on his mind. As long as Missy got the hint.

She glanced at him, but looked away quickly.

"I guess there is something you can cook." Brent spoke in Missy's ear, so the others wouldn't hear him tease her.

She narrowed her eyes at him, while trying not to smile. Her lips quivered before she gave in and shrugged.

"Pie anyone?" Dale asked, adding to Missy, "You have to try my apple pie."

"I'll try to fit in a piece."

Brent could see her surprise when she bit into the first bite. "Can all the men around here cook and bake better than me?"

Brent liked Dale's pies, but what he really wanted for dessert was the woman sampling a bite. He watched her savor it, her eyes fluttering shut, and then opening to look right at him.

A blush crept up her neck and onto her cheeks. Brent's manners insisted he didn't rush everyone out the door after dinner, but his body couldn't wait to get Missy alone.

On that thought, he cleared the table and let his company talk. Glancing back at them, he saw Missy's gaze on him. His legs. She worked her way up and seemed to stop right below his belt. He let out his breath when she moved on to his stomach. She lingered there, too. Then his chest.

She was chewing her lips. Someone help him.

Finally she looked up at his face and went flaming red. *Oh, yeah, baby, I'm watching you, too.* He smiled.

Rubbing her neck, she turned back to Alice, who wore a sly smile.

"Well, I think we need to be getting home." Alice spoke loud enough for Dale to hear her as she stood. Ivan sat with his wife on the couch, about climbing in her lap, so he looked equally pleased with the idea.

Missy's face had gone from red to pale. He'd let her leave if she gave the slightest indication she wasn't ready to be close to him. Maybe he scared her. He'd gobbled her up with his gaze all night. Where had his self-control had gone? Right in the gutter, along with his thoughts.

Dale and Alice wished everyone a happy Thanksgiving and left. He knew they'd exchanged a look about the heat between him and Missy. But hell, he couldn't hide it. He'd never wanted anyone like this before, and he didn't care who saw it.

After Ivan and Tina drove away, Missy turned to him with questioning eyes, her mouth parted.

"I didn't mean to make you uneasy tonight," he started. She looked down and he felt like kicking himself.

"Maybe it wasn't you." She looked up again. He felt a leap of excitement when he read the feelings there. "I'm not used to feeling like this."

*Let me touch you.* He felt like a boy on a cliff, staring at the deep water below. *Jump, and it'll be over.* But he didn't move yet.

"Want help cleaning up this mess?" She glanced around, a hand on her neck again.

"I didn't get you alone to clean." He pulled her into an embrace without thinking or questioning it. "I've wanted to kiss your neck all night."

His mouth made her moan, and she leaned her head back. Brent trailed his mouth up to her ear and his hands slid into her hair. The clip holding her hair up popped.

She didn't care. *Kiss me!*

With one hand, he brushed her hair over her shoulder and slid his hand down the silky length of it. Since their bodies were pressed together, he felt her body heat through her clothing. It made him want to feel that heat skin to skin.

They mirrored smiles at each other when her head tilted back to look at him. Heaven help him, he couldn't hold back with her.

"Missy . . . if you don't want to kiss me, you'd better run now."

"No way. I'm staying." Her brown eyes held desire, not fear. He saw the cloudy look in her eyes, and brought his mouth down on hers. Soft, warm, and ready. To gain her trust, he kept the contact light at first. But she parted her lips in an invitation.

He felt like he took flight as she melted into him, molded every inch of her to his body. Clinging to him, she welcomed his advance, meeting his tongue. Urgency to devour her overwhelmed him.

Her sweet kiss turned passionate. She tilted her head, wrapped her arms tighter around his neck, and kissed him with the same wildness he felt.

He deepened the kiss when she moaned, but then she hesitated. Pulling back, he saw her open her eyes to meet his gaze. She looked both amazed and puzzled.

Murmuring, he asked, "Friends can kiss once in a while, can't they?"

"I'll allow it today." She looked at his lips and leaned forward. Without looking away from his mouth, she ran a finger across his top lip, then bottom.

He imagined pushing her back on the couch and kissing her breathless. But he needed her trust.

"I love your mouth." His words came out a whisper.

Suddenly her mouth landed on his, her body against him. She shocked the socks off him by slipping her hands under his shirt and spreading her fingers across his stomach.

She chewed on his bottom lip to drive him crazy. The kiss deepened.

She pulled him with her and fell back on the couch. "Touch me."

Had she somehow seen his fantasy in his eyes?

"Are you sure?" He didn't plan on pushing things. She didn't answer, just grabbed his hand and pulled it against her. So she wasn't an uptight city girl, but an adventurous siren.

Had she ever seemed like a city girl? A loud knock sounded at the door, causing him to pause.

She clung to him, shaking her head. "Don't answer it."

What could be so important? He hadn't felt an earthquake. He didn't smell smoke.

For the life of him, he couldn't pull away from her. The knock got louder, then Dale called his name.

"Damn it all!" Brent jumped up to answer the door, saying over his shoulder, "He'll walk right in here if we don't answer."

He threw open the door to scowl at Dale. "Is something on fire?"

Dale looked baffled. "You better get out here, the stable roof's leaking. We've got a muddy mess in there and some unhappy horses."

Dale left before Brent could grab his coat. Missy rushed to come with him.

"Listen, you don't need to be out in the cold and wet." He didn't think she'd know how to help anyway.

Her dark gaze held his, looking determined as heck to go with him.

"Fine, I don't have time to argue." He turned toward the door, and she followed him into the dark night. The rain fell slow enough to look like snow, but it wasn't cold enough for that.

After several steps, he thought about how he'd spoken to her. Looking over, however, she didn't look angry. "Listen, getting interrupted like that . . . it, uh, it doesn't feel so great. Sorry I snapped at you."

The corners of her mouth rounded in a smile. "Forgiven. I'm not too thrilled, either. That's why I didn't want to sit there by myself."

Really? He wanted to tease her, but they were close to the stables.

Dale placed a ladder against the side, with the tools close by.

"I'll hold, you go up first," Brent directed Dale. Missy stepped back as Dale climbed. Brent turned

*A Cowboy For Christmas*

to her when Dale reached the roof. Her head went back to look up, and she looked scared.

He chucked the rolled-up tarp up and made sure Dale caught it, then he picked up the toolbox to take up with him.

"Hold the ladder for me?" Judging from the look on her face, she didn't like heights. He wasn't about to ask her to come up.

"Okay, go."

He didn't rush since the ladder was wet, and he had to perch the box on a rung, take a step, and then move the toolbox. He reached the roof and looked down through the darkness.

"I'll go take care of the horses," she called and disappeared in two seconds flat. He'd have to laugh about it later, when the horses were dry.

The lone flashlight he'd thought to bring didn't do much in the way of lighting. Dale used his own flashlight to light his workspace. With the rain and tilted roof, it wasn't a fun job, but they got it done.

"Missy!" He had to bellow her name out since she was still inside. She ran out and understood he wanted her to hold the ladder. Once they were both on the ground again, he said, "Let's survey the damage."

With only five boarder horses, their total came to fifteen, and Missy had moved them so every horse was in a dry stall.

"I wonder why a little water set them off." Dale rubbed his beard.

Brent shrugged since there wasn't any way to tell, but he noticed Missy had gotten the horses into dry blankets for the night.

"We'll take care of this," Brent told Dale. "You can head on home."

Dale nodded to them on his way out. Missy had been quiet and he turned to her now. "You have a way with them, you know. They're settled down like nothing bothered them."

She didn't answer, and he knew she was thinking over what had happened between them in his house. The woman sure did like to think things over.

"Warm enough?" His coat had gotten soaked through while he hammered the tarp down.

"I'm good. We'll be done soon anyway." She started back to the wet stalls. "This isn't so bad. It'll dry now that new water isn't dripping in."

"Let's head out, then." He waited for her to turn around and look at him, but she didn't. She started for the door.

Curious reaction. "Would you like to come back to my place?"

Now she turned. "I . . . I'm not sure."

He didn't plan to push things, not when she looked worried about something. "Okay, I'll walk you home."

At his words, her shoulders relaxed and she tried to smile. His instinct had been on, but what scared her? He put an arm around her on the way, and was grateful she leaned into him, accepting his comfort.

They hurried through the rain. Not that they could get any wetter.

At her door, he asked, "How about you and I go out tomorrow night?"

She didn't hesitate on that one. "Sure."

Maybe she just needed to take it slow. Now under her porch roof, he rubbed her wet hair. He pulled her chin up and sank his mouth onto hers, finding her lips as cold as his own. He kept the kiss light and added another to her forehead before sending her inside.

Once her door was shut, he headed home, not caring about the cold drizzle coming down or the stable roof.

\* \* \* \*

Missy stood facing her bathroom mirror when she heard Brent's truck. No time to change her clothes again. Still nervous about taking this step, she didn't wait for him to knock, but grabbed her jacket and purse and walked outside to meet him on the porch.

Memory flashes from the night before hit her, once again sending desire through her. She'd kissed him until she couldn't think.

He stepped out of the truck, looking dangerous in his tan cowboy hat, a crisp dress shirt, and his long legs in new jeans. Dangerous to her hormones, that was. He looked so good she ignored the flowers.

He checked her out, up and down. Then again. "Guess you're ready."

He looked dumbfounded, but she didn't find it as funny. Another time, maybe, but now she just liked knowing she did that to him.

She met his gaze. "I heard you coming and didn't want to wait inside." She took the flowers he handed her, brought the red roses to her nose, but she wasn't expecting them to smell so rich, deep, and somehow of love. "Come in and I'll put them in water."

She turned and took them with her, letting him follow. *Like the view from back there?* He seemed so entranced by her. She was aware she had some curves, but his adoring eyes, and hands, took her unprepared.

She arranged them without making a fuss so they could go. He'd stayed by the counter while she poured water and set the vase down. But she smelled his cologne, felt his presence.

She looked up. He watched her, too, his lips parted and his eyes aglow with something like sentiment or reverence. Whatever it was, it stopped her from moving or breathing for a full minute.

He swallowed and she shook herself. So that was what it felt like when the world stopped. She took his hand for the short walk outside into the chilly night to the truck. It was still running, so the inside was warm.

"How did today go?" It'd been the first thought and she needed something to stop her escalating emotions. How could he get her so worked up?

"We got the roof done." He looked over to answer, and she was pretty sure he looked down to her breasts and then to her legs.

She smoothed her hands down her skirt, glad she'd worn the short skirt, even if it was winter. "That's good."

"Nervous?"

"We're being honest about it?" She didn't want to answer, but that answered for her. Could he be nervous, too? With his calm exterior, she had no way to tell. Even when he took on jumpy horses or tall ladders, he didn't look nervous.

He turned on the radio to a country station. There were a lot of things she could discuss with him, but the lack of conversation felt nice for now. Maybe he already understood she was thankful when he backed off the night before. She'd been so ready until she had time to think about it.

It wasn't that she needed time. She just liked to think things over. And she had. Quite a lot.

He pulled into the restaurant parking lot and turned off the engine.

"I get to open your door for you." He jumped out and came around. She'd never seen the point in that type of thing, but she had to admit she liked it when he offered his hand. "Did I tell you how beautiful you look?"

"Thanks." She linked her arm though his. "I thought you might appreciate something besides Wranglers."

"Now, you can't knock Wranglers. Especially if you could see your cute little butt in them." He gave it a pat before grabbing the restaurant door. The unexpected touch left her skin tingling. Inside, they were seated right away despite the dinner crowd.

She studied her menu, but noted he studied her curves. She'd worn a burgundy top with lace at the neckline. It swooped down lower than her work shirts. Combined with the skirt, it seemed to get his attention.

"Our waiter is coming." She set her menu aside. "Did you decide?"

"Oh, yeah, I know what I want." The pure appreciation in his eyes let her know it, too.

She tried not to blush as the waiter approached their table. Brent turned and ordered, knowing what he wanted though he hadn't looked at the menu. It sounded so good, she ordered it as well. Alone again, they both smiled, staring.

"I take it you don't offer trail rides in the winter." She decided to talk about the ranch, a safe subject.

"Not yet. There's several stables along the coast that do, and they're much bigger. We take their overflow in peak season."

"Do you plan to expand?" She'd controlled the urge to ask this kind of question before, in case it brought back the tension.

"I'm sure we will someday. And I guess you have a say in that now." His tone wasn't cold. But they were on thin ice, she knew.

"I still want to know what you planned." She wanted to be a part of the stables and the plans, not take over.

"I saw a vision of the place, and that's pretty much what it is right now. I have the land, the horses, and the beach nearby." His gaze dropped down to the table. She didn't think he was mad, but he was closing up in himself. Something was off.

Ben.

They hadn't spoken much about her late brother. She couldn't hold it against him, since they hadn't known each other for a long period of time. Things were going well enough for her to want to stay on longer, and he seemed to want that as well.

Something, however, still dogged him. Why else would he avoid Dancer? Why else would he clam up when she asked about the future?

She remembered the one and only time she had asked him about Ben's death. He'd refused to answer.

Switching gears, she asked, "Do you think I'll be able to help with the tours this spring?"

When his face came back up, his eyes were clear. "I plan on it. Two of us always go with every group, maybe more if it's a large one. One leads the way, the other brings up the rear."

He'd worked with Ben before. She could tell he didn't want to talk about it. His hand rested on the table, and she reached over and covered his with her own. He didn't pull his hand back, but stroked hers with his thumb.

"You seem to have a lot of confidence in me," she said. It gave her a warm feeling, but she didn't want his feelings toward her to cloud his judgment on this.

"You still have time," he reminded, still stroking her hand. "For your first few times, three of us can go. It'll work out fine. I can tell by watching you ride now."

Their meals arrived and they ate in silence. They'd planned on a movie afterwards, but she couldn't sit next to him in the dark and watch a movie. "Would you like to go to my place for wine?" she asked as they walked to the truck.

He must have seen right through that. Teasing her, he said, "Didn't you just have wine with dinner?"

After he opened her door, she slid in and waited until he sat behind the wheel to ask, "Then would you like to come back to my place and kiss me?"

"Just one kiss?" He started the truck and put it in reverse. The music played and she scooted in the middle for the trip back. He smelled like pure pleasure, she thought as she leaned her head against his shoulder. She was a sucker for his wide shoulders.

"Missy?"

She shot up at his questioning tone. "Yeah?"

"Thanks for . . . for the way you are."

What could he mean by that? "My sultry good looks or my amazing charm?"

He chuckled. "I like a woman with a good self image." He rubbed her with the arm he had wrapped around her. "But I meant for your understanding. I thought you'd change everything. Now I'm not sure why I was so against you coming here."

She could remind him that he'd just lost a good friend, and she came looking for money. But she didn't just remember those things. How could she forget how hurt and angry she felt?

"Wasn't the best way to meet, was it?" she said, her voice quiet and sad.

He turned down the ranch road, passing under the *Ocean View Stables* sign, passing his own house and drove to hers.

"You're not leaving once you drop me off, are you?" Oh, boy, that sounded like panic in her voice. After all her daydreaming, she needed him in the most intimate way.

"I'll stay, go, do whatever you want."

That innuendo didn't escape her notice. And after looking at him, she knew he meant it. Time to put it to the test.

"Come on, cowboy." She started to slide over to the passenger door.

His hand on her arm stopped her. "It's closer this way."

Surprised, she turned to him just as he pulled her up into his arms. "Let's hurry, it's cold."

He took her right in and set her on her feet inside the front door.

Shutting the door behind her, she leaned against it, looking into his blue eyes and then that mouth waiting to take hers. Powerful urges burned inside her, keeping her from moving.

"Missy?" His voice washed over her, making her shiver. "Are you cold?"

She shook her head and watched him step next to her. He touched her cheek, her neck, and leaned in to kiss her. Moaning, she fell against him and wrapped her arms around his neck. His face was just a bit rough under her lips. Enjoying the texture, she ran her lips over his whiskers.

In contrast, his neck felt like silk, right down to his collarbone. She undid the top several buttons of his shirt and ran her hand over the thin chest hair underneath. She shivered with pleasure. While she wanted to touch every inch of him, right now, she needed to savor. The last buttons went and she pushed his shirt open.

She'd thought a lot about trusting him with this. If she thought he'd understand, she'd tell him what a big step she was taking. To understand that, however, he'd have to know why she was afraid to trust. Shame kept her from doing that.

His hands sculpted her waist, running down to the dip before her hips. She could trust him this way. Her heart would be another matter.

"All this comes off," she told him with one brow crooked suggestively.

"Does it?" He threw her up into his arms again and carted her back to her bedroom.

*Kristen N. Bailey*

## Chapter Eight

Brent hadn't slept that good in ages. Walking to the stables in the soft morning light, he felt renewed. He might have slept better if he'd stayed with her, but he'd gotten the sense she wanted him to leave. They had lain together for a while, until he was about asleep, when she pulled away.

Since he wanted to respect her, and continue to build her trust in him, he'd dressed and headed for home like that was the natural thing to do.

It wasn't his natural reaction. He'd wanted to hold her all night, listen to her breathe, and kiss her neck in the morning. He'd never felt love like this before. Wait. Love?

Love. That was the only word for the overwhelming emotions raging inside him. It'd been in there somewhere, hiding, waiting for the right second to spring itself on him. Then, suddenly, while holding Missy and making love to her, he knew.

He might have even said it out loud. If he did, she hadn't heard. That was a miracle. How would he explain that to her?

"Morning, Dale," he said and wished he hadn't sounded so happy. If Dale noticed anything, he was gentleman enough not to ask. With the sun coming out, Brent felt like spring was coming early.

They transferred the horses to the back section of the pasture. The recent rain had started a puddle that turned into a small lake.

He waved to Dale and went back for his truck. He needed to make a run for sawdust before the pasture got any worse. When he returned, he spent an hour spreading sawdust. H stood back for a break when Dale pulled up with another truckload of it.

"We could just keep them off this section." Dale looked over the mushy mess, his mustache twitching.

"We'd still have a mess come spring." There'd be even more rain then.

"Here comes Missy," Dale jerked his head her way. "To help, I think."

Brent turned around to see Missy walking down to them. She wore rubber work boots with a pair of Wranglers and a heavy coat.

"Cute, isn't she?" Dale grinned at him. "So you two getting to be pretty good friends?"

"It's way past being friends." He allowed himself one knowing look directed at his friend. "But I don't kiss and tell."

Dale tried to wiggle the smile off his face before Missy got there. "You just did, buddy."

With Missy several steps away, all Brent could do was send Dale a warning look to keep quiet.

"Want some help?" she asked by the truck.

"Couldn't hurt." He watched her come the rest of the way over, but she didn't look his way. He'd expected at least a shy smile. Nothing?

They worked together and talked to Dale like things weren't different between them. Coldness settled inside him. Dread of loosing what little they had scared him silly.

*A Cowboy For Christmas*

They emptied the truck in half an hour with two extra bodies. Dale acted overly excited about leaving for lunch. Maybe he felt something off with Missy, just as Brent had.

"Let's take the horses out." He took her shovel and laid it in the truck bed.

"A ride, now?" she asked, like the idea was from left field.

That tone seemed too normal after the night they'd shared. He opened the passenger door and guided her in. Like it or not, they were going for a ride. And they were going to talk.

With her brows creased and her lips parted, she looked startled when he got in, but maybe he needed to shake her up a bit.

He steered the truck down to the stables and parked it. Missy jumped out and headed for the tact room. She could saddle her horse like nothing now. Just like anything else around the stables that needed done.

She'd promised to learn fast. And she had. But maybe he was a slow learner because he was missing something here.

"Ready?" she asked from atop her horse. He mounted and nodded.

He rode close to her side as they took the path into the forest. The breeze rattled the pine branches, sending droplets down like rain. Didn't matter. They were dressed for wet weather.

"All right, no one's listening. What's going on with you today?" He hadn't meant to sound so demanding. Did he care, though?

"Is there something you should tell me?" she said, concern in her voice.

"You're acting different." He nudged Jeffery closer.

~ 111 ~

"I've been thinking about last night."

This wasn't good at all. Maybe she had heard his confession of love, and it had scared her off. That or he wasn't any good in bed. After the way she moaned, he doubted that was the case. "Second thoughts?"

"No." She laughed, looking him over from his boots to his hat. "Reliving it. I didn't want us going all goo-goo in front of Dale."

He let out his breath in a half laugh.

"Don't worry so much, Mr. Serious Cowboy." She lifted an eyebrow at him and turned the serious discussion into play. Trotting ahead, she glanced back. "Coming?"

He'd never heard a laugh like hers. Quiet, yet suggestive. Relieved, he kicked up the pace and caught her.

They came back muddy and soaked, but he hardly felt it. Even the horses didn't seem to mind. He brushed them and checked them both over.

"You sure take good care of these horses." Watching him, she patted Speckle.

"Some might think I overdo it." He turned his back to pull up Jeffery's hoof. "But it's best if you catch things before they fester."

He straightened and found her face had gone serious.

"You thinking things over again?" He didn't need to think after watching her ride. He needed to kiss her all over.

"Oh, I'm thinking about Dancer."

Dancer. Guilt spiked through him at the horse's name. "Yeah, I'll ask Dale to take him for a ride soon."

He couldn't go near the horse, couldn't think about Ben. Or that day when he should have been driving the truck and trailer. He felt how she watched him. This wasn't the time to tell her.

"You sure got dirty." He grinned at her muddy clothes. Sure, he had to force the grin, but she relaxed.

She fluttered her lashes. "Maybe we need a bath."

He grabbed her hand so quick, she gasped. He whipped them outside and straight to his house.

"Brent?"

"You said you need a bath." He lifted one side of his mouth, then looked her over. Talk about hot.

He threw open his door and pulled her inside. She tried to kick off her boots, but he yanked her into his arms.

He pulled off his Stetson and dropped it on the floor. Their lips met, hers feeling hot against his mouth. The clothes were in his way, so he pushed her coat off her shoulders.

She moaned into his mouth as he kissed her. Pulling his hands back, he jerked his coat off, tossing it over his shoulder to land on the floor behind him.

"Bathroom," he growled.

"You're serious about this, aren't you?" She murmured and took a step back. She crossed her arms, grabbed the bottom of her shirt, and pulled it up and over her head in one motion.

Have mercy! She let him stare at her white satin bra for about ten seconds. Then with a spin, she left for the bathroom. "Did you want to join me?"

"You little tease!" He reached the bathroom in five fast steps.

She giggled. "And you love it."

She had him there.

"Maybe I should do some teasing." He grabbed her and turned her to face him. "With my tongue."

He didn't look away from her pleasantly surprised face when he kicked the bathroom door shut with his foot.

\* \* \* \*

Lying in Brent's bed with him, she couldn't believe how satisfied she felt. He'd shown such care while rubbing the towel over her and taking her to his bed. Before she met him, she wouldn't have thought the same man could match her need in the bedroom, then be patient and caring to her once their passion was spent.

"Seems you've decided to stay on," he said, low and quiet. That's what he'd been thinking about? She lay on her back with the sheet pulled up to keep her warm. Under the sheet next to her, he leaned up on his elbow so he could trace his finger down her neck.

"I knew I would from the beginning," she corrected. "I said I would prove myself, and I knew I could make it."

He shook his head, a half smile coming and going. "I did, too. I knew you could make it, but I didn't know if you'd want to stay."

Why else would she go through all this trouble? Just to leave? Something happened in his past, but what? "Brent?"

"I didn't know what would happen here. If you stayed or went on your way . . . we were short a worker." He kept his gaze off her face while he spoke, and only glanced up now as he paused. "I didn't want to replace Ben, and I couldn't hire anyone. So you had more power than you knew."

"I didn't think of it as power. I wanted to make it here, to show I could." And she had, hadn't she? Pride filled her. It hadn't been easy to come here, stay and learn how to share in the work.

He'd been teasing a finger over her skin, but now he pulled his hand back. "Are you staying now that you've proved you can do it?"

For the first time, she heard uncertainty in his voice, and he lacked the hard confidence he'd displayed since she met him. This wasn't about the ranch. She asked, "Haven't I proved that?"

She couldn't hear him breathing. What was going on with him?

"Is that your answer?" he asked.

She felt him tense next to her. "I'm not going anywhere. But I can't make promises about you and me. We don't know what we want from each other, if this will turn into anything else."

She couldn't let it become something else yet. Russ had whispered sweet things to her, made promises, and he'd been wearing a mask. Even while she felt her trust for Brent grow, she didn't trust herself to recognize a lie anymore.

"Are you afraid it will?" He broke into her thoughts, touching her arm again.

She was sleepy and didn't want to talk about this. "There's no point in trying to predict the future." Right as she spoke the words, she felt a jolt. The future had been so uncertain for her when she came here. Was it still?

She just wanted to be held, but he wouldn't do that now. Her own words made her realize that while she wanted to have plans, she was afraid of setting herself up for another crash. She'd come to love life here. When she thought about risking it for a relationship with Brent, her stomach went flipping over in circles.

After a silence, he said, "I think you're afraid of a lot of things. Sometime, I want to know what those things are."

That couldn't happen, she wouldn't let it. She sat up and said, "I should get going before I fall asleep."

\* \* \* \*

*First things first.* Brent stood outside the passenger side door of his truck at daybreak. In one hand, he held a lighter. In the other, he held the will Ben had started to put together. Ben hadn't been the type to think ahead. That had been Brent's part in this venture, so he never expected Ben to have a will.

It gave Missy only a one-fourth interest in Ben's share, while the remaining three-fourths went to him.

Last night, Missy had shown him she wasn't ready to put her roots down here. Why was she unwilling to plan? To talk about their future? He sure as heck wouldn't give her a reason to take off.

Holding the will at arm's length, he lit it.

Ocean View Stables had been his dream, one that he'd made into a reality. He still planned on directing it, choosing where they'd go. And Missy would be a part of it.

He dropped the flaming document and watched as it burned down to a crinkling paper before he stomped it out.

Missy wouldn't be up this early, so he went back to his place for breakfast. He was lost in thought, waiting for his toast to pop up, when someone knocked.

Missy stood outside, looking sleepy still in sweat pants and a big coat.

"You could have stayed here, you know," he reminded once again, shaking his head at the woman. Why bother taking off during the night if you're coming right back in the morning?

She yawned and came in.

"Toast?"

A nod.

"Coffee?"

Another nod. She sat on a stool at the counter and laid her head down on her arms. Since she looked asleep, he let her be. Why had she come back instead of sleeping? It didn't make sense, not after she'd wanted to take off the night before. He dropped more bread in the toaster and started fresh coffee. She hadn't moved.

That couldn't be comfortable. If she had drifted off, he intended to move her to his bed, whether or not she liked that when she woke up. "Are you asleep on my counter?"

"No." She rolled her head and opened her eyes. "You get up this early?"

"Why didn't you just stay?" He didn't get it, and that made him mad.

"I don't do that."

"You always sleep with guys and take off?" That went over the line. Turning his back to her, he grabbed the fresh toast and buttered it.

"I don't sleep with guys. So I didn't know what to think."

His hands stilled. Her words and tone told him he'd come on too strong, asked too much of her.

Now what could he do about it? He didn't want to back off.

Bringing two plates of toast over, he sat opposite her. "I just made a jerk of myself. I don't do that kind of thing, either. Haven't in a long time."

She looked awake after that comment. They chewed on toast for a minute before he grabbed two mugs and poured coffee. "Sugar? Cream?"

"Please. Lots of both."

He dumped them in, added just cream to his, and sat again. He wasn't ready to let go of their conversation. "I could help."

"With?"

"You've asked about plans for the stables, but you won't talk about our future. You take off after we make love. I think there's something I should know."

"No," she said and looked down at her mug and took a quick, jagged breath. "Unless you want to talk about Ben. About Ben's horse and why you avoid him."

Jarred and unprepared, he said. "One topic at a time, sweetheart."

"Don't you think they're related?" She raised her gaze finally, and he saw fire in her eyes. Why did she care about that? It didn't affect their relationship, not like her secrets did.

He wanted to answer, but didn't know how to say anything that could end this. They stared each other down as unease settled over them like the fog outside the house. Were they in too deep?

She downed the last of her coffee and stood. "Listen, we're great in bed together. Why mess it up? Obviously, we're not ready to share the other parts of our lives."

Turning, she went to the front door and left. He wished he could run after her. He did want to share everything. The ranch. Their lives. Their secrets.

But he didn't know how he could tell her about his part in Ben's death.

*Kristen N. Bailey*

## Chapter Nine

He'd give Missy her space. They both could use time to think.

He just missed her, and didn't want to consider his reasons for clamming up.

Because two boarder horses were leaving that day, he couldn't talk to Missy in the morning. After loading the horses into the trailer, he paused outside the driver side door. He didn't think anyone had noticed how hard it was on him to drive the truck with a trailer behind it.

It was the one moment when he couldn't push it away.

After that dark moment passed, he climbed into the truck and started it. What would Missy think if he told her?

He transported the horses back to their owners, who had returned from vacation, then picked up more hay while he was out. He wished, as he looked over at the passenger seat, that she would have come along.

He wanted to slip over and see her for lunch, like they'd done many times now, but he needed to think about what he'd say. So he went back to his own place when he was done working. After heating up leftovers, he chewed without tasting, wondering how he'd gotten so lost.

After lunch, he ventured to Missy's door. Maybe she wanted to forget about last night.

While taking her porch steps, he brushed off any lingering hay, before looking up to find her standing in her open door.

"We sure complicated things before," he said. Maybe that was why she'd left instead of staying with him.

The soft skin around her eyes wasn't red from crying, but her face looked gloomy today, and her brown eyes dark. She stepped inside and let him follow her in.

When she stopped and turned to him, they were inches apart, and her eyes grew heavy with need. The change threw him, but only for a second, because he always needed her.

He swept her into an embrace, barely getting the door shut behind them while he hungrily kissed her.

"You look good," she said, pulling off his coat to see his thick, cotton shirt underneath.

"Work clothes." He gently pulled the band from her ponytail to set her long hair free.

"You look good when you work."

He tugged on her shirt, but she made him wait till they were in the bedroom to pull her clothes off. Both were naked in minutes.

They fell onto the bed in a rush. Her body was made for his hands, the curves and dips, the swells. Their tense words were forgotten in their kisses. She seemed to need him as much as the first time. When she arched up against him, it sent him over the edge.

"Sorry," he gasped against her neck. "You got the better of me."

She laughed under him, shaking them. He ran his fingers through her hair, pulling it to his nose to smell her lavender shampoo.

*A Cowboy For Christmas*

"Missy."

"You sure like saying my name in the bedroom." She said with a smile, gazing into his eyes.

Did he? What else did he say while making love to her?

"Because you like having me in your bedroom so much." He rolled so they lay stomach to stomach and skimmed his hand over every inch of her. "Do we have time for round two?"

"What else do we have to do today?" She followed his lead and flattened her hand on his chest before running it all over his bare skin. While he'd been nice and touched her sensitive places, she teased and ran around his.

With a sly smile, he said, "The new horse will be here in an hour."

"Oh!"

"Did you forget?"

"Not until you showed up at my door." She continued to tease him. "A lot can happen in an hour."

His body responded to her hands. What if the owner brought the horse early? Didn't matter, he couldn't move. "Do I make you forget things?"

"Let's find out!"

\* \* \* \*

Forty minutes later, they were scrambling to make it to the stables in time. Brent would have never guessed he would enjoy watching her dress. She'd yanked on her jeans and a sweater and pulled on a navy coat to protect her from the biting cold outside. A cold front had interrupted their mild weather, but at least it wasn't below freezing.

As they walked together down to the road, Brent heard a truck rolling toward them on the gravel.

"We made it just in time," Missy said when the truck pulled up with the horse trailer behind it.

"Mr. Henderson!" He greeted the horse's owner when the truck door opened. He'd picked up the horse before, but Henderson seemed nervous about leaving him this time.

Stepping out, the older, thin man nodded at them both. "Hello, Brent."

"This is Missy Nelson. She's running the place along with me now," he introduced her, not caring if the way he did it implied they were more than business partners. They were, whether or not she wanted to see it that way.

Henderson flicked a thumb back towards the horse. "He's anxious over this trip. So if he gets too rowdy, please call me. We'll turn around if this doesn't work out."

"We can handle it. I've had tense hoses here before without any problems." Brent motioned for Missy to help lead the horse out of the trailer.

"Well, Jumper here is a Draft Cross, so I didn't expect him to . . . well, fit his name the way he does. We love him, but he's a handful. And the trip over shook him up pretty bad."

Brent let Jumper smell his hand while he petted its muzzle. "Seems calm enough now. I can put him in a stall, if that's all right."

"Well . . . he's been in the trailer two hours longer than I planned. Our road turned into a mud pit last night, and I had to do some digging on the way over." Mr. Henderson rubbed Jumper's neck. "He might like to get out and stretch."

"Alright. Come on, big boy, time to stretch those legs," Brent said as he led Jumper out into a partitioned pasture. He expected Henderson to stay and watch the horse at least a few minutes, but he looked at his watch and said his family was already waiting for him.

"That mud threw off our schedule. I'm sure you're right. He seems right at home," Henderson said as Brent closed the gate to the pasture.

They waved when Mr. Henderson pulled his truck around the circle and headed out.

"So you think he'll calm down?" Missy asked as she watched the truck drive down the road.

"Seems to be doing fine now," Brent answered. "We'll just keep him away from the other horse. And us, as much as we can help it. Let's give him room."

Together, they each hitched a foot on a wood beam of the fence and watched the horse adjust. Brent slid a sideways look at Missy while she focused on the horse. Most folks without previous horse experience would be greenhorns still. Not this lady.

While she still had a lot to learn, she'd proved how easily she could learn it. She might not be able to guess at a horse's sickness, but she'd feel something was off. That intuition was the best start she could hope for.

Within minutes, Jumper had circled the area and was now running and bucking. Brent got chills up his back, but tried to shake off the unease starting to form over him like wet dew.

"What happened?" she asked him. "He's acting up again."

"He got scent of the mares." He watched the new boarder with unease as he bucked around his section of pasture.

Missy watched Jumper, then threw Brent a worried look. "I'm not sure Jumper and the fences are getting along."

"The good news is that's flexi fence on the back half, and it won't hurt a horse like wood railing would, if they hit." Brent paused. "But I'm starting to wonder if he can jump them."

No, he didn't like this one bit.

"Can you calm him down or should I bring in the mares?" Three mares grazed in their own pasture, but it touched one corner of Jumper's.

"He's spooked." Brent straightened. "Stay back if he gets out of control. I'll get him into a stall to calm down."

\* \* \* \*

"Don't get hurt," she called to Brent before turning away. Not wanting to watch Brent with Jumper, she entered the stables to see if Ivan had mucked out a stall for their new arrival.

Inside, she stopped when she saw Ivan leading Jeffery to a new stall. "What's going on?" Brent didn't have anyone else care for his horse.

"I'm almost done with a stall for the new horse. But Jeffery's upset about something, maybe that new horse out there. I'm moving him further down."

That seemed like a good idea, but just then Brent came around the corner to lead Jumper inside. She felt uneasy about the situation, especially when she saw Brent's eyes go cool and calculating. Straight fear shot up into her stomach.

"What's Jeffery doing out?"

"Ivan's moving him." She backed away from Jumper as he pawed the ground. Now closer to Ivan and Brent's horse, she hoped to help guide him away from Jumper and back into a stall.

"All right, I'm taking Jumper back out for a minute." Brent turned Jumper to leave just as Jeffery reared up. Missy flattened against the wall, praying no one would get kicked.

"I lost him!" Ivan exclaimed in a panic laced voice. She knew better than to get underfoot as Jeffery charged to the exit.

Something *clanged*. Jumper bucked, but Brent kept hold of his reins.

Still, the horses faced off with wild eyes and flying hooves. Jeffery gave a startled horse screech and charged past.

"Jeffery!" The horse didn't slow his pace even as Brent called out. He wrestled Jumper into a stall, slammed the door and took off at a run to find Jeffery.

She knew she couldn't help with Jeffery, so she tried to soothe the agitated animal they'd just penned. She talked to Jumper the way she heard Brent talk to the horses. "That's right, boy, settle down. Everything's okay."

"Is he hurt?" Ivan asked from behind her.

"I don't think so. Stay with him a minute."

She rushed outside and spotted Brent. Jeffery hadn't made it far. He was injured. He stood by the fence, a hind leg lifted, as Brent approached.

"Hey, boy, it's just me." Brent took slow steps, coming up to Jeffery at an angle. He held out his hand toward the horse's nose. "Come on, boy. I need to see your side."

She stayed still to give them space while Brent settled him down. She could make out the wound on Jeffery's side, where his stomach and hip met.

Ivan walked up beside her, and they watched Brent from the stable entrance.

"This isn't good," she whispered to Ivan. "Jumper kicked Jeffery. See by his hind leg?"

She glanced at Ivan and saw the horror on his face.

"It was just a misunderstanding," she added. As bad as things were, they could have been much worse. She valued the horses, but not over Brent.

She watched while Brent looked over his horse and called the vet on his cell phone. After squeezing Ivan's shoulder, she walked halfway to Brent and the horse.

"Can I help?" she offered, but he shook his head - a quick, don't bother me shake - without turning to look at her. All right, it was his horse. She backed up to the stables, trying not to let her anxiety show.

Ivan looked nervous too, so she suggested they clean up in the stables. A few things had been knocked over, and the horses were making noises.

Dancer snorted when he saw her, his way of calling her over. Ivan turned and saw her pet him.

"You two getting along now?"

"Yeah, we like each other, don't we?" She'd made the effort and he'd warmed up.

The worry in Ivan's face added to her own.

"Why don't you go home to Tina?" she suggested.

Turning, she came face to face with Dancer. "Hey, there, boy. It's okay."

He pawed and made noises that she'd come to think were for agreement.

Night fell outside and the temperature dropped. She sighed and watched her breath in the air.

Would Brent be upset with her what happened? She didn't know if anyone was to blame, or maybe they all had needed to work together better.

She laid her face on Dancer's muzzle. She enjoyed their friendship as he made soothing noises to her. Then, at the crunch behind her, she guessed Dancer had chosen to let Brent walk up unannounced behind them.

She glanced up and found Brent's eyes were soft, questioning. He'd already taken his jacket off, and pulled it around her shoulders. His cologne surrounded her, underlain with the smell of his skin. She hugged it close while turning to him.

"Is Dancer calmed down?" That quiet voice of his washed over her.

"He's doing good, and we're friends now." She turned to the horse again, afraid to look at Brent's eyes because she needed to see something there, and she wasn't sure she would.

"Missy." His whisper made her pause, and his arms wrapped around her and pulled her back against him. She could see their breath in the night air. "Come back to my house with me."

That wasn't anger in his voice. It was flat out desire.

"Okay." She patted Dancer before leaving. Brent put his arm around her. Shock ran through her at how much she needed him.

"It'll be alright."

His words put tears in her eyes, but she hid them by pressing her face closer to him. What had happened today? It felt like more than an accident occurred.

In his bedroom, he trailed kisses all over her body while he undressed her. She felt the need he always sparked, but her heart ached with strange emotions. Unable to speak, she clung to him for comfort and warmth and the fulfillment he offered. Spending their mutual need left them entwined in each other's arms. Cassie wasn't sure who was holding who, but she needed his arms around her.

"Today reminded me of the day Ben died," Brent said softly. His words were soft, but she jumped into alertness, her heart thudding hard.

Why hadn't she seen that?

Raising her head, she looked into his face in the dim light. "Today wasn't your fault. Neither was that day."

"You weren't there."

She didn't care what the facts were. "Tell me what you're thinking."

He shrugged, and since they were lying down together, his shoulders moved under her. "I lost control."

This must be the male mind at work. She wouldn't argue now, but just let him talk. "Of your horse, you mean?"

"I wasn't clear enough to Ivan. I didn't give enough weight to Jumper's mood. I should have checked before bringing Jumper into the stables."

She wanted to say *what's done is done*, but that wouldn't help him. This was the first time she'd seen this side of him, one that worried and admitted weakness.

"Jeffery will recover, won't he?" She grabbed unto that because she didn't see any way to relieve Brent's guilt.

"He'll heal."

So why couldn't Brent let go of it? They'd all learned something. She almost pointed out that she was more to blame, but he'd feel bad for that, too.

"How did you lose control when Ben died?" she asked instead. She couldn't have asked this before, but he'd brought it up this time. He wanted someone to listen, she could tell that much.

After several deep breaths, he said, "I could have gone. I planned to, but he didn't want to wait. So he went and got in the accident."

She could see why it was hard on him, but he didn't cause the accident or make Ben drive the truck that day. "You didn't ask him to go?"

"No, but I should have just gone."

"You can't change the past." Wow, big revelation there. That should help him out. "I don't think it was your fault, and I don't think Ben would want you to regret that day for the rest of your life."

What would he say to that? He didn't answer, but pulled her closer to him. She laid her face on his chest and listened to him breathe.

He seemed to be waiting for something. What else could she say? Minutes ticked by and he didn't go to sleep, but rubbed circles on her bare shoulders with his hand.

She wanted to ask what he wanted, because she felt stiffness in his shoulders. With a jump in her heartbeat, she remembered what he wanted. Another conversation came to mind, the tense talk they'd had that morning in his kitchen. She'd asked him to share then, and he had demanded the same from her.

Now what? Her heart took off running, and she wanted to bolt from the bed, too. She noticed his heartbeat was running a little fast as well while he waited for her to say something.

This wasn't something she could throw out there on the spur of the moment. She didn't know if she could ever tell him.

Several slow and tense minutes passed before he sighed. They didn't speak again, but he didn't let her slip away that night.

\* \* \* \*

Brent woke up early and smelled lavender. He'd lost it if he smelled her when she wasn't there. And felt the warmth of her bare back pressed against his front.

He wasn't remembering her scent, he smelled her. There, with him, asleep. Hugging her closer, he breathed in her scent and kissed her cheek, her neck, that little spot where her neck met her shoulder. His face fit perfectly. Their bodies fit just right as they lay there together.

The night before crashed back into his thoughts, like the waves beating the beach. A throb started in his temples. Had he asked too much?

He'd opened his heart, expecting her to do the same. What could be so big and dark that she couldn't tell him? After all they'd shared, she couldn't trust him the way he trusted her.

Maybe she didn't plan to stick around.

As she made a little noise, she turned to him. When her eyes opened and he saw uncertainty there, his stomach knotted up. "Missy . . . will you be all right today?"

She nodded, flattening her hand on his chest.

"Will you come to me if you need to talk?" he asked, and she nodded again. That nod didn't necessarily mean she'd talk to him about whatever hurt her before.

Holding her, he kissed her face and reassured her before getting up. Seeing her in his bed made him feel torn between his responsibility for his horse . . . And the woman he loved.

She wanted space. He could see it in her desperate look. "I need to go down to the stables. But you can stay there as long as you like."

Nestled down into the covers like that, she had her face half hidden and didn't give away anything in her expression.

"Thanks," she said when the moment drug out. He took her hand and reluctantly let go to leave. What could he do with a woman like that? He loved her enough to let her get away with it. But he knew she'd eventually need to talk about it.

He could tell that Ivan was expecting to get it for the incident. The young man readily agreed to check on the horse during the night and the morning before Brent could make it over. He didn't bother saying anything to Ivan, knowing it wasn't needed. Some things in life weren't learned through words.

He went to the stables and to his horse. "Hey, old friend. Just couldn't let that other horse show you up, could you?"

The soft footsteps surprised him. He'd expected Missy to stay in bed a while or find something to keep her busy. So far, she hadn't felt the need to spend all her time with him.

Maybe she was here to talk to him. It could happen, just like he could win the lottery or find gold on his property. He turned to look at her while still running his gloved hand over Jeffery's nose. She wore a sheepskin coat, her hands tucked into her pockets. With her long hair pulled back into a ponytail, she had a strange aloof look that didn't go with her personality.

Something was stirring in the air, and he got a bad feeling about it.

In the minutes while he waited, he caught her quick glances.

"I have to ask you something." She'd kept the distance between them, and he could tell this was hard for her to do.

"Shoot," he said. Guilt flashed through her eyes, filling him with dread.

She pulled in a breath, taking forever. "We have to cool things between us."

Out of all the possible requests, he hadn't seen that coming. Though the air hung misty and silent around them, her words seemed to echo in the cold.

"Brent?"

"Why?" *Why do you want to gut me and leave me to die?*

"The ranch." She tried to shrug. "My sanity."

He stepped closer, wanting to take hold of her arms, but she backed up. "I can tell you're lying."

"What do you know?" That city girl cover was back, the one she'd worn the day she came to his porch.

"Is this about what I told you last night?" he asked, confused and hurt that his confession would drive her away.

With a shake of the head, she said, "Of course not. Don't ever think that."

"Then what? Don't you see I need you? I think you need me." Brent stepped so quickly, she couldn't back away from him. She couldn't run with his hand gripping her arm, but she didn't look like she planned to answer him, either.

Eyes big, she bunched her mouth up at him. "I don't *want* to need you." Her enraged voice told him she was telling the truth for once.

"I don't understand. I know you didn't plan on this, but neither did I. Fate brought us together."

At the fiery flashes in her eyes, he knew he'd picked the wrong words.

"Are you saying I don't have a choice?"

"Of course you do," he said, wishing to hell he could understand her. "I just need to know why you won't take it." Why couldn't he break through?

She shook her arm free. "I can't walk into this lightly. I need to think about it."

In his opinion, she did too much thinking, but he let her leave.

*Kristen N. Bailey*

## Chapter Ten

The radio on her kitchen counter played Christmas music, but to Missy, it didn't feel like Christmas would be coming to Ocean View Stables.

Telling Brent the truth had seemed like the worst thing that could happen. Maybe she couldn't handle this.

"Time to make peace." She stood in her kitchen, watching out her window as Brent walked with Jeffery in the pasture. After two weeks of not talking with him, not working beside him, or making love to him, she felt like a stranger to herself.

She wrapped up in a coat and scarf and walked down to see him, knowing he might send her packing. He saw her coming, but didn't give her a warm greeting.

"How is he?" she asked, not stepping close enough to pet Jeffery.

"Much better, thanks." He only gave her a glance. Boy, he wasn't going easy on her, was he?

"I missed you," she tried. He whipped around, sending her a step back.

"I didn't send you away, remember?" She'd never heard his soft voice sound as bitter as it did now. Had she hurt him that badly? "You wanted to cool things down, they're cooled."

She pushed her hands deep into her coat pockets to keep them warm. "I got scared."

"And I offered to help." He kept his attention on the horse and she stood for several minutes, thinking about leaving. But she couldn't. He sighed and turned to her. "You want me, then you don't. My horse is more dependable than you are."

"Okay, fine," she mumbled to herself on her way into the stables. She decided Dancer needed some one on one time with her. It'd be good for both of them.

Maybe a horse *was* more dependable. So what? Why did she have to be dependable? She saddled Dancer and took off on the path to the top of the hill. They set a good pace, stopping when they arrived at the spectacular view of the Pacific Ocean.

Waves rose and fell in a natural rhythm and pace. The cold wind stung her cheeks, but she welcomed it.

Such a beautiful view . . . she loved this place. She wasn't sure when it had happened, but she felt like she was home – like she'd found whatever it was she'd been looking for.

She nudged the horse and headed back as the sun slipped down into the clouds over the water.

\* \* \* \*

After she'd put Dancer up, she trudged back to her little house in the fading light. Inside she flipped on the lights and dropped onto her couch. Was there enough wine left in her fridge to get her drunk? She was almost in tears, about to get the wine, when someone knocked.

Knowing it'd be him, she opened her door to a tall cowboy, his hat in hand, and hurt in his blue eyes. She had put that hurt there, and that made her stomach go sour. She let him in and went back to her couch.

"What's going on, Missy?"

"I was wrong." She could say it only so many ways. He looked so handsome. And so frustrated.

"Is this about Ben?"

She stared at him, dumbstruck. "Oh, you're mad at me. I replaced him. And you're mad at me."

His eyes went wide. "No!"

Then what did he mean? She waited for an answer. He turned his hat in his hands. After a sigh, he said, "I don't know what else to think. You won't give me anything."

Actually, she'd given him everything but the truth. "Sit down with me, Brent."

He sat and immediately demanded, "If that's not it, what's holding you back?"

She couldn't break eye contact. His blue eyes held hope and questions. He'd shared his guilt with her, why couldn't she tell him?

She hadn't said the words out loud to anyone. And she stared at him now in silence, her heart pumping erratically in her chest. Each beat sounded loud inside her, hurting. Each breath took effort.

She'd give anything for him to know, to somehow read her mind, and save her from saying the words. She couldn't do it.

"I can't do this, Missy." He stood and her heart shattered. "If you want me, you want me. And if not, we'll see what happens here at the ranch. But you can't go one way and then the other."

His eyes blazed at her as he set his hat back on his head. He stormed out, maybe for the last time.

* * * *

That couldn't have gone worse. After stalking out into the darkness, he stopped and stood with both hands on his hips. He'd do anything to get Missy to love him, truly love him and share her life and secrets with him.

What could it be? What haunted her and kept her so guarded?

A light rain began to fall as he stood in the middle of the road. Rain didn't bother him. The expression he'd seen on her face when he left did.

Now walking just to move, he took one step after another, though he didn't want to leave. Was fair the most important thing? No matter what else happened, he couldn't leave things be the way they were. He loved her, even if they didn't have a future together, so he couldn't leave her with those angry words.

Halfway back to his house, he couldn't go on. He turned and started for her house again, but right then he heard someone take off from the stables on horseback. How'd she get past him?

Did that woman take to a horse every time she got mad?

He ran to the stables, threw a saddle on Jeffery and took off after her. The rain continued to drizzle, coating him with tiny water droplets that started soaking through his clothes. At least she'd stuck to a path, so he saw her up ahead.

"Missy!"

She turned Dancer to run off, but he galloped up to her. She really meant it when she said her

*A Cowboy For Christmas*

and Dancer were friends. At least someone was riding him again.

"Wait, Missy, can I tell you something?" He could barely see her.

"I deserve it, so go ahead." Her rough, shaking voice told him what his eyes couldn't.

"I didn't mean to tear into you that way. I said what I did because I care about you." He paused, wanting to stop, but he couldn't hold back his feelings for her. "I love being around you, but I can't do it, not if you're this way."

"What way?" The rain had flattened her hair to her face and down her shoulders, but she didn't seem to notice.

"I'll put aside the fact that you're out here alone on a black night." He wanted to tell her to get inside, but they had more important things to discuss. "You were into me, now you're running. You're breaking my heart."

Her horse became still. Missy, too, remained quiet, and he had to take that as her signal for him to leave. Fine, he'd had his say and she wasn't stopping him. "All right, Missy. But please get inside. You'll get hurt out here."

He retreated a ways down the path and made sure she got back to the stables, figuring she knew he was keeping an eye on her. How could he not? She could tear his heart in two, but he couldn't control how much he wanted to protect her. He waited outside while she took care of Dancer before he took Jeffery in and brushed him.

\* \* \* \*

For two full minutes, Missy stood outside Brent's cabin door with her fist raised to knock. *You're breaking my heart.* She'd never broken anyone's heart before. She'd never had anyone who cared so much about her. After he said that, she couldn't stay away.

The door swung open before she knocked.

"I'm sorry." She wrapped her arms around herself. "For the way I've treated you. I've been immature and selfish. And confused." His face was set and hard, his brows creased as she stared at him. She pulled in a breath, but it sounded like a sob before she finished.

"Come here." He grabbed her by the arms as he spoke and pulled her against him. They embraced with her chin tucked into his neck. "I don't care what you do anymore, but you better not ever run away from me again."

"What if I hurt you, Brent?" She liked how he felt against her and how his arms held her close.

"You didn't drag me into this."

"But what if I'm using you so I won't be alone for the holidays?" In truth, that had been one small consideration. But she couldn't tell him the rest.

"Is that so bad?" He ran his hand down her hair and rested it against her cheek. She wondered if he was letting her off the hook about telling him the truth. He added, "Sounds like you don't want to hurt me."

"I'm scared I will. And that you'll want more than I have to give you."

"Right now, it's more than enough just to hold you." He pulled her closer so that she could feel his warmth through their layers of clothing. "I can go slow, follow your lead."

"You make it sound easy," she mumbled, closing her eyes.

"I'm trying, I don't want to make your life harder than it is."

"I'm the one doing that. My life's about as simple as you can get. I make my own hours, run things the way I want to. It's the stuff inside me that's messing up everything."

"I don't think it is." He pulled her head back to look into her eyes. "The only suggestion I can offer is to share your burden. When you're ready, I want to help you."

His expression sent shivers through her. He touched his forehead to hers with his eyes closed. His lips touched hers, moved, and took on an urgency until she couldn't resist.

She answered him and wrapped her arms around him, pulled him as close as possible, and didn't fight the feelings stirring up inside.

"I love you, Missy, and I can't fight it." Speaking against her cheek, he shut the door behind her and looked into her eyes. Love? That couldn't be what she was feeling. What about trust?

Her heart pumped with a painful velocity, and she knew if she didn't share, it'd end up hurting her. "It's about time I told you a few things." She took his hand. "About me."

\* \* \* \*

Brent knew he couldn't walk away from her, no matter how big this turned out to be. He pulled her into the living room and onto the couch with him. "Whatever you want to tell me, I'll still love you."

"I don't doubt that." She sighed. "I don't feel good about myself while holding this back." Tears flooded her eyes. "This is about the job I left behind."

Things clicked together in his head, and he couldn't believe he hadn't seen it before. "This is about the man you dated there."

"Russ, my boss." She met his gaze. "He flirted with me from the day I started working for the firm. But I didn't want to date someone from the office." Her voice shook so she paused. "He was persistent."

He nudged the tears off her cheeks with his knuckles. "So you never dated?"

A stalker? Harassment in the office? No matter how the jerk scared her, he'd have to pay.

"Yes, we did. I've been ashamed of it ever since." She stared straight down at the floor, but looked up when he touched her. "I finally went out with him just because he'd been asking for so long. He seemed to care about me, and I hoped I might feel something for him if we went on a date." She stopped, looking down again, and he noticed she was barely breathing.

"Missy?" He scooted closer, wrapping his arms around her. "What happened? I remember you said he fired you."

"My feelings didn't change, and he grew more and more pushy. Then, one night when we were alone at the office, I told him I didn't feel anything for him, that I couldn't sleep with him, and that I couldn't date him anymore."

And he sent her packing. Brent tried to imagine how that made her feel, and could understand why she'd been so reserved when she came to the ranch.

"He wouldn't accept that." She spoke so quietly that he almost missed what she *wasn't* saying. Gently, he touched her chin and nudged her face his way again. She turned her head but didn't look at him.

"There's more, isn't there?"

"He thought the security guard was done with his rounds, but the guard was running late. If he hadn't been on the floor, and heard my yells, Russ would have raped me."

Pulling her close to him, he saw their time together in retrospect. Certain things, strange before, now made sense. After pulling in a deep breath to calm his rage, he asked, "Did you report him?"

"I ran. I went home and tried to figure out what to do, but I couldn't think. By the time I called the police two hours later, they already had a report. Against me."

"You?" He stiffened.

"For stalking Russ. They told me I was lucky they didn't have enough to press charges, but they were going to watch me. By morning, the entire office had heard that I offered him sex when he fired me."

"The bastard. He's enjoying his high paying job, and you left town."

"No one's going to hire me now."

He felt her tears through his shirt and pulled her even closer. "We'll make it right, Missy."

Instead of answering, she rubbed her face into him, still crying. He didn't know what he'd do to the man who tried to hurt her, but he sure as hell wasn't going to let him get away with it.

"So that's what this was about. You had good reason not to trust me, or any man." He rubbed her back, wanting her to release the tears and held-back emotions. "I'd sell this ranch before I hurt you. I'd give away the horses, move into a city."

That'd be hell for him, but still not as bad as losing her. When her breathing sounded normal, he kissed her temple.

His lips trailed down to her neck, making her fingers dig into him. She couldn't hold still. "It's been so long." She almost cried the words.

"Too long," he agreed and felt her body tremble, come alive. She reached out to him and he knew that by sharing, she'd freed herself of the guilt that held her back before.

"Don't torture me." She pulled him back to her mouth roughly. His hands, resting on her shoulders, pushed her jacket off and slid down her side to rest on her hips. All of her, he had to touch all of her. He lost his breath when her hands slid under his worn T-shirt. Her touch did things to him; things he hadn't known were possible. "Missy," he murmured into her hair.

\* \* \* \*

Later, when his breathing slowed, he rolled onto his side, taking her with him, so they lay facing each other. After soothing her hair away from her face, he kissed her once more.

"You're smiling," he whispered.

"So are you."

"Guess we're both happy. That's a good thing."

A good thing. She shivered as her body cooled. Brent pulled the covers over them and drew her near.

He pulled her close and held her. They didn't speak. What they'd shared could mean so many things, or nothing.

*A Cowboy For Christmas*

"Have you noticed we resolve arguments with sex?" she asked.

"Not sex. We make love." He pulled her chin up and looked into her eyes. "In case you haven't gotten it yet, I love you."

"I know." Her eyes were warm with love, but he wasn't sure she'd tell him any time soon. Then she surprised him. "I'm not sure why it's been hard for me to say that. I heard you the first time, you know. I love you. I have for a while."

"Stay with me tonight."

In response, she moved closer.

*Kristen N. Bailey*

# Chapter Eleven

"Thanks, Nick." Brent hung up the phone. Standing by the kitchen window, he looked out at the horses in the pasture, but his mind was on everything Missy had told him. Nick Hatcher thought they could do something legally about it, and agreed with Brent that men like Russ were repeat offenders.

And now he would have someone checking up on him. If Russ had tried to hurt anyone else, Nick Hatcher would find out about it.

The clouds parted outside and bright sunshine shone in through the large windows. He spotted Missy walking up the pasture, in her red jacket and scarf, her hair whipping in the wind. The temperature had taken a nosedive, but that wouldn't keep them inside.

After yanking on his own coat, he met her at the bottom of the steps. She smiled and took the arm he offered. He spun her around and planted his mouth on hers. When he finished he lifted his face.

She smiled. "Mmm . . . what was that for?"

"Your lips needed warming up." He grinned at her. When they had decided to go out today, she had asked him for things to be normal. He decided not to tell her about calling Nick just yet. That way she could enjoy today.

"Race you!"

He hadn't expected that. She was halfway to the stables already, and he couldn't move as he watched that little bottom of hers.

She turned at the stable entrance and held her hands out in a question.

"Why run when I can watch you?"

"Like my legs, huh?" she asked, trying not to smile.

"And everything else." He caught up to her and they went back to the tack room together. Once their horses were ready, they rode out into the forest.

"Are you looking forward to Christmas?" Brent asked. He remembered how little excitement she'd shown about Thanksgiving . . . until the actual day. Now out in the forest, they dismounted and walked slowly. She ducked under a wet Douglass fir branch, eyes scanning the smaller trees growing at the edge of the clearing they stepped into.

"I am, I think." Side by side now, they looked through the trees around them. "I haven't done much for the holidays in years . . . How about that one over there?"

He ignored her first comment, since she seemed to want to skip over it, and stuck to business -- the business of picking out a tree. He sized up the six-foot tree, imagining how he'd trim it into the perfect shape. Thinking of the holidays made him think about family, think about him and Missy that way.

"Brent?"

Oh, no, he'd let his face get too serious. But had to ask, "You sure you don't want a tree for house?"

till think of it as Ben's house."

He paused because she did, too. "Ever consider staying with me?"

"You? Aren't you too old for a sleepover?" She giggled with her face turned the other way, cluing him in. She had understood what he meant, but he let that go as well.

With her gloved hand up in a branch, she paused and studied him. "I like this tree, Brent, and I want it in your living room."

Shaking his head and smiling at the same time, he pulled the saw from behind his saddle. She walked his way again and watched him work.

Feeling her behind him, he asked, "Enjoying the show?"

"Yes, very much, thank you."

The tree tilted to one side as he sawed through it. "Timber!" Water drops sprang out of the tree as he shook it and threw it into the long wagon they'd towed behind his horse.

"I love that chilly tree smell," she said, then took a deep breath of it before she smiled at him. Their gazes were on each other as tiny snowflakes fluttered between them.

When she tilted her face up and let the flakes flutter down on her, he couldn't breathe. He stepped in and wrapped his arms around her. A million sensations exploded inside him, especially when he heard her gleeful moan.

\* \* \* \*

Stepping into Missy's place, Brent still didn't know how he'd tell her what he'd done. Or that Nick had called him back with news. Too bad he couldn't put this off. He wanted to spend the holiday with her without this monster on their backs.

"Smells like heaven in here," he greeted, trying to keep a light tone.

"Heaven smells like chocolate chip cookies?" She turned to see him staring at the cooling batch of homemade treats. "Some are plain old chocolate . . . And some are white chocolate with macadamia nuts."

"Winter Wonderland" played from her CD player to set the Christmas mood. A happy scene and he might have to ruin it. Might have to? There wasn't any way around this.

She slid a glass of milk in front of Brent. "Remember the first day I met you?"

He nodded, thinking of the slick woman who'd shown up in his drive. Smooth on the outside, anyway, but her eyes had given her away. Deep brown and mournful, like a lost puppy.

"You poured me a glass of milk. I thought it was pretty funny after the way you treated me."

"Mmm, mmm." He'd bitten into a cookie as she spoke, so he couldn't answer right away. "Oh . . . you looked so worn and tired."

"Gee, thanks." She nibbled on her own cookie.

"You looked hot, I won't deny that, but you just looked like you needed something." He decided not to tell her about the puppy comparison. She might not bake him any more treats if he did.

"You think I'm hot?" She dipped her cookie in milk and nibbled.

Watching her mouth, he said, "Hot and ready to take over my ranch."

"I wasn't after your ranch." Her voice lowered to a husky drawl. Brent sent the rest of his milk down, following his cookies, and stared at the glass while deciding how to tell her.

*A Cowboy For Christmas*

"Is something bothering you today?" she asked before he could even start.

"That obvious, huh?" He raised his gaze to meet hers. "It's about you, and what you told me. I talked to Nick about it."

"What?" Her brows raised and her eyes widened.

"I can't hear something like that and not do anything." He should have seen this mess coming. Too late to reconsider now.

"Why didn't you at least ask?" she demanded, holding her hands palms up. Tears of hurt swam in her eyes, slamming instant guilt into his gut. She added, "Why Nick?"

Maybe now he could explain. "He's a lawyer. I didn't tell him to gossip about you. I wouldn't do that to anyone. I asked him to look into this Russ thing."

Her nostrils flared and she planted her hands on the edge of the counter, like she needed something to hang onto. When she blew a breath out her mouth, he stepped closer.

"Don't close up on me, Missy," he pleaded, wrapping his arms around her waist and leaning his face onto her shoulder. He'd done this to her, and he'd hold her while she worked through it. She could push him away, but he wouldn't leave.

On a sob, she asked, "What am I supposed to think?"

"How about justice? Getting your good reputation back?" he asked, just as his own tunnel vision hit him. If she got this mess cleaned up, she could return to Las Vegas and get another advertising job. Had he just given her the perfect out?

Once again, too late to consider that. He loved her and had to do this for her, no matter what happened between them.

She hadn't answered, so he said, "Missy?"

"What do you want? Do you want me to press charges? Pull my humiliation out again for everyone to see? He lied, I have nothing to stand on. Especially since I ran."

"You do!" He twirled her around and brought their faces close. "He's been indicted for sexual harassment. You can add your say in with the other women who are pressing charges."

Her mouth fell open and new tears sprang into her eyes.

"Yeah, sweetie, the truth's out. Everyone knows what a scumbag he is. And he'll pay for hurting you and others." He pulled her into his arms.

The strength of her sobs and her body shaking took him by surprise. He saw that he hadn't fully understood what this had done to her.

Even if she left his life, this would always be there. He'd hold onto the fact that he'd helped her. He'd given her something.

"It's all right now. Everything will get fixed," he murmured into her hair. Holding her felt so good, he pushed away the urge to ask her if she'd stay.

* * * *

A fire blazed in the fireplace as Brent paced in front of it, waiting for Missy. Weren't they done yet? He should have stayed with her while she talked to Nick and the detective. So what if she didn't want him there?

Okay, he had to respect her wishes, even if it tore him apart. He wanted to be there for her now.

The phone rang. Would she call from her place and tell him to come over?

"Hello?"

"Is Miss Nelson available?"

Nerves prickling, he asked, "Who's calling?"

When he learned it was the firm Missy had worked for in Las Vegas, his nerves settled. But something else awakened. "Can I also tell her the reason for the call?"

"That depends upon who you are."

"I'm dating her," he declared without a thought about it. They were doing something, even if they'd never defined it. "I know what's going on, and I don't want you harassing her."

"Of course not. After we learned what happened with Russ Faraway, we'd like to make things right. We're offering her a job, with a raise, of course."

Well, there you go. He would lose her for sure now. After the phone call, he couldn't pace around his living room, waiting for them to finish. He grabbed his coat and slid his arms inside of it on his way down his front steps.

At her house, he rapped on the door and opened it. Inside, he found Missy sitting at her kitchen table with both Nick and the detective.
Nick stood. "Hey, Brent. This is Detective Anderson."

"Hey," he said while all three looked at him. "Missy, he said, "Your old firm called . . . to offer you a job."

"Oh."

He could tell she didn't know how to react. Nick and Anderson watched her, waiting. At least Missy knew why he'd come right over. This meant leaving the stables, leaving him.

Missy knew he'd been afraid of this very thing happening.

After glancing at the men sitting at the table, she asked, "Did the person offer to call back? Or am I supposed to call them?"

Call them? Now he had a delayed reaction. Staring at her, he didn't want to believe what he'd heard. "I gave him your number."

Even with his gaze trained on Missy, he could tell the other two men were looking between the two of them. The room felt too small.

While he gazed at her, wondering about her decision, she simply stared back at him with a slight frown. She seemed to be searching his eyes for some kind of answer. Didn't she want to stay with him?

Life without her would be like days without sunshine . . . a sky without stars . . . he'd live his life without any *life* in it.

She wanted the job. He'd feared this, but he didn't expect it.

His world didn't feel right. And to think, he'd handed this right to her by calling in his lawyer. Everyone still stared at him. After he nodded at them, he turned and left, walking down to the stables.

Dale was headed that way, leading a horse back inside. "Hey, what's up?"

His tone of voice asked what was going on, why Brent was dashing down there like God himself had sent him. Without breaking stride, he said, "I need something to do."

"Got plenty of that." Dale muttered after him.

He worked a good two hours before saddling Jeffery. It was mid December and biting cold, but he didn't care. Hardly felt it as they cut through the fields and took off up into the hills.

He didn't want to think about the stables without Missy around. Maybe she'd come back to visit, but that would be more heartache.

He felt out of control once again. He couldn't make her stay. He wouldn't want to make up her mind for her.

But he sure as hell wasn't going to sit back and not fight for her.

\* \* \* \*

The man mystified her. Didn't he decide to dig into this? Didn't he call Nick and ask him to check up on Russ?

She walked along the main road, her hands stuffed deep in her coat pockets, while a cold wind pushed at her back. Why did Brent go to all the trouble he did, then avoid her? Did he want her to accept the position in Las Vegas and leave the stables?

Before she learned about the job, she'd already decided she wouldn't stay unless he wanted her there. If he loved her.

When had that become the issue? She kicked a rock and turned toward the path to her front door. Inside, she picked up the phone.

He didn't sound happy when he answered.

"Hey . . . do you still want me to decorate your tree with you?"

"What are you waiting for? You don't have to call," he said, his voice sounding more like him. She hung up a minute later, her chest hurting. Her heart hurt.

She loved him.

Did he know that?

She walked to his house. When he opened the door, he pulled her into his arms and kissed her, but it felt like he held back.

During the last three days, she'd had trouble finding him. Maybe he thought they were over and this was a goodbye for him.

No, she couldn't think like that. With his arms around her, she nuzzled into the soft shirt he wore and breathed in his smell.

"Come on, I've been waiting." He led the way to the tree, which stood in front of the window in the living room. It stood in the stand, but without any decorations on it.

He kissed her cheek and said, "I'll get the decorations."

She went to the fire while waiting for him. She loved this house, and would miss it if she had to leave. But not anything like how she'd miss Brent.

Music came on and she turned. He carried a huge box over and set it on the floor in front of the tree.

Joining him, she sat while he opened it. She expected him to ask about the job offer or how the trial was progressing. A date had been set and she had a rough idea of when she'd need to fly to Las Vegas to testify. Brent, however, didn't seem interested. Not enough, anyway, to ask about it.

Or was he afraid? He didn't look at her like he normally did, and remained quiet as they hung ornaments together. Most were plain globes of red or green, but a few were unique and he told her about them.

Other than that, they didn't talk. The daylight faded by the time they finished.

"It's beautiful. Just needs the lights turned on."

*A Cowboy For Christmas*

Walking behind the tree, Brent plugged it in and light sparkled forth. It sent colors across the carpet that blended with the glow from the fireplace.

Standing still before it, she stared at the picture it made. She wanted to see his face, to know what he was feeling, but he'd moved back. When she turned, he was laying a blanket out on the carpet.

"Would you like a glass of wine?" he asked.

Taken back by the blanket and his question, she mumbled, "Sure. That'd be nice."

Wine? A blanket? She'd missed something. Maybe he wasn't mad at all. Maybe he didn't want her to leave. Or maybe he wanted to make love one last time before she did.

He returned and set their glasses on an old chest before sitting down. "Come on, join me?"

They sipped wine and looked at the tree. The fire warmed her, and so did sitting next to him. Longing filled her . . . for something more. She'd come to the stables and found a home, but suddenly felt something lacking, especially as she thought about the holidays.

He lay down and gave her arm a small tug.

"Do you think it's silly?" she asked, leaning back into the crook under his arm. He'd spread the blanket almost under the Christmas tree, so she could look up into the lights.

"Laying here with you? What's silly about that?"

"I meant the tree, the season."

"Silly? Celebrating family and being together? No."

Leaning on his elbow, he looked at her with such love. He showed her everything inside him

~ 159 ~

and looked all the more manly because of it. His strong mouth so temping . . . she brushed her hand down his narrow face, the face she dreamed of at night and thought about during the day.

"I love you, Brent." She'd caught him off guard and watched his face grow soft, his brows lift.

"Missy, I love you so much it wakes me up at night. I think your name in the shower and have to suck in a breath. I'll never get you out of my system."

Tears came to her eyes. She loved him so much, it felt like it'd always been there. She pulled his mouth to hers and kissed him deeply.

He pulled his mouth an inch back from hers. "I have to give you one present early."

"You have no choice?"

"No, ma'am. The law says so." He rose and reached for her hand, pulling her to her feet and a step closer to the tree. Still holding her hand, he guided it under a branch near the top to a small box.

How had he hidden it there? The film of liquid in her eyes grew into round tears and rolled over her lashes. She wiped at them. Once he'd settled it into her open hand, she studied it for a long minute.

"Open it." His whisper brought her back to reality. She slipped the delicate ribbon off and pulled the top open. Little flares of color reflected off the solitaire.

"My word, Brent. Did you sell all the horses to buy this?"

He choked back a laugh, dropping down to one knee. "Missy, I love you and I want to marry you and spend my life with you."

The tears in her eyes turned the light reflecting off the diamond into streaks. Wiping her eyes, she nodded.

"Is that a yes?"

"Did you ask a question?" She teased him right back, but didn't laugh.

"Will you stay here? Don't go back to Las Vegas. Stay with me, be my wife."

"I'd like that. I never planned on going back, not since I set foot on this place."

\* \* \* \*

If the couple in front of the Christmas tree noticed the lights and the people around them, it didn't show. Missy stared into Brent's warm and loving eyes and the preacher lead them through their vows.

"I do," he whispered, never looking away. She loved his blue eyes, his face, his lips. And now she could look at him every day for the rest of her life.

When her turn came, she said, "I do."

His lips touched hers, and shivers of joy ran through her. The kiss deepened and her heart quivered. She wrapped her arms around his neck and kissed him like she couldn't live without him.

Cheers went up. Both Brent and Missy smiled at their guests. She felt so happy seeing the people she cared about around her to share this moment. Through the toasts and laughing, her heart swelled as she watched her new husband. And her body ached for him. When their gazes met, the blaze in his eyes said that he felt the same.

And it showed when the last guest left and Brent swept her into his arms, kissed her neck, and carried her to the bedroom.

"Aren't you supposed to carry me across the threshold?" she teased, murmuring the words against his mouth, against their kiss.

"You look like you want the bedroom right now!"

"I do, I do!"

Each kiss held tenderness and forever love. "You're my wife - you're staying!" he exclaimed with his arms wrapped around her. Brent laid her softly on the bed and kissed her left hand. She looked down at her wedding ring as he kissed up her arm. Slowly, he undressed her, kissing her body all over until she lay naked.

Her stomach flipped with excitement while her body buzzed with love. She ran her hands lightly over his muscled back, finding his body both familiar and exciting. He, too, memorized her body with his hands in a worship of love.

"Remember when we first met?" he asked, looking into her eyes.

"How could I forget?"

"Well, it's true . . . I'd never forget a face like yours. I'm so glad you showed up that day."

She rose onto one elbow. "And fell in love with you?"

After a smile, she kissed his lips lightly. He gazed in to her eyes and told her, "You mean everything to me, Missy."

"Good, 'cause I'm sticking around for good!"

Kristen Bailey loves to watch wildlife in her yard and on the river by her house. She's been writing since grade school and now works as a full time freelance writer, author and book publisher. Her articles appear on eHow and other sites, and she placed in the 78th Writer's Digest Writing Competition with an excerpt from *The River People* – an adventure story set in the Pacific Northwest featuring the culture of Native Americans.

Besides writing, she loves cycling, fishing and camping. Luckily her three children share her love of the outdoors and they enjoy different adventures together.

Email her at admin@kristen-bailey.com and visit her website, www.kristen-bailey.com for updates on new books and events.

The Herald and News of Klamath Falls called The River People "A nicely told tale that discusses American Indians from a different perspective. It combines history with romance, with a hint of early women's liberation, and a larger dose of Indian culture."

Sometimes her reporter instincts get Cora Evans in trouble. This time, she learns her father is in danger. Helping him throws her in the middle of criminal family and on a "paid vacation" into the wilderness.